Green Mountain,

White Cloud

Green Mountain,

White Cloud

A Novel of Love in the Ming Dynasty

FRANÇOIS CHENG

Translated from the French by Timothy Bent

St. Martin's Press ✿ New York

www.stmartins.com

Library of Congress Cataloging-in-Publication Data

Cheng, François.
   [Eternité n'est pas de trop. English]
   Green Mountain, white cloud : a novel of love in the Ming Dynasty / François Cheng; translated from the French by Timothy Bent.—
1st U.S. ed.
      p. cm.
   ISBN 0-312-31574-0
   EAN 978-0312-31574-0
      1. China—History—Ming dynasty, 1368–1644—Fiction.   I. Bent, Timothy.   II. Title.

PQ2663.H3913E8613 2004
843'.914—dc22
                                                        2003066806

First published in France under the title L'éternité n'est pas de trop by Editions Albin Michel, S.A., 2002

First U.S. Edition: April 2004

10   9   8   7   6   5   4   3   2   1

Green Mountain,

White Cloud

Prologue

YEARS AGO I ATTENDED A CONFERENCE AT ROYAUMONT, A medieval French abbey located outside Paris in a beautifully maintained park. The abbey provided an ideal setting for the conference, the point of which was to promote harmony among cultures. The interlocking, hand-hewn stone blocks of the venerable old structure, the vaulting branches of the ancient and majestic trees—everything seemed expressly designed to inspire mutual understanding and respect. Here was a place where minds and spirits might unite through dialogue. We are not made of stone or wood, after all; we are creatures of language.

Genuine dialogue between people, and by extension between cultures, truly is a rare thing. To achieve it, we have to transcend appearances and dive deep into ourselves, down to where those fundamental questions reside that ultimately we must ask both of one another and of ourselves. Everything depends upon the sincerity of the replies. Only when they are sincere do they measure the ways in which we are alike and differ, and then—after we have summoned as much humility as we are able—help us to accept the distinction and learn from it.

Anyway, I had been invited to this conference to speak about China, from which I had emigrated some years earlier. Before undertaking to talk about the life and culture of my native land, as well as to lend some freshness to my reflections, I felt a need, nearly a physical ache, to reread some of the old Chinese texts whose voices and messages I had absorbed so long before. Even better would have been to become acquainted with books I had not yet read. Thus when a conference organizer happened to mention in passing that one of the abbey's spacious rooms housed a large number of manuscripts that had been brought back from China in the 1950s by a scholar in residence there and now deceased, it seemed a nearly miraculous coincidence.

I was shown into the room in question and stood in amazement. Stacked on shelves and tables were dozens of old texts, each in its distinctive pastel-colored jacket and exuding a familiar odor of dried herbs. I flipped through several at random. Bound with fine thread, the paper was supple and soft to the touch. Many had annotations in the margins. These seemed to be suggestions for translating key phrases and passages, and were quite extensive. The scholar must have spent many thousands of hours poring over these books, trying to master the meanings of their mysterious characters, far from home.

A quick survey revealed that he had been most interested in the Ming Dynasty, for there was a substantial number of

François Cheng

books dating from that period, and on a desk lay copies of articles he had written about it. He had chosen well, this old scholar.

Stretching from the mid-fourteenth century to the mid-seventeenth century, the Ming had supplanted a dynasty founded by the Mongols and established an era of rigorous and implacable formal order. During the latter half of the dynasty, however, roughly from the middle of the sixteenth century to the first decades of the seventeenth, the populace, in equal measure to the increasing corruption of their rulers, longed for change. The growth of cities and towns and of commerce gave rise to a precapitalist kind of economy. Moreover, until then, China had had contact only with India and Iran, due to the Silk Route. Ming rulers had launched ambitious exploratory sea expeditions, so the country was starting to become acquainted with the countries of South Asia. Frequent attacks along the coastal provinces by marauding Japanese pirates impressed upon the Chinese the importance of this neighboring land. And finally, it was during the Ming period that European culture, then in the full flower of its Renaissance, began making inroads into China, chiefly through the determined efforts of Jesuit missionaries.

Someone reflecting on the future of contemporary China might be tempted to see this earlier era as an encouraging precedent. Following the collapse of the Han, around the third century, China, thrown into chaos, had been fertilized by influences from outside, in this case the introduction of Buddhism. During the Tang (618–907) and North Song (960–1127) Dynasties, it underwent a remarkable cultural transformation. Because of its articulation of the nature of sin and the accompanying concern for the state of the soul, its notions regarding the stages and the states of meditation, and its general embrace of charity, Buddhism brought something radically new to Chinese thought.

By the time of the Ming, these profound changes had spawned a generation of highly independent thinkers, notably those from the Taizhu School, such as Wang Gen and Li Zhi, who revolted against conventions. Other intellectuals followed their lead and then took matters further. Wang Fu-zhi, Gu Yen-wu, and Huang Zong-xi went so far as to question the very legitimacy of the imperial system. Literary giants arose, Zhang Dai and Li Yu, for example, both of whose works contain highly individualized forms of inspiration and expression. Increasingly, stories and novels contained descriptions of reality and psychological analyses of character. Changes were also reflected in painting, most notably among the so-called eccentrics, such as Chen Shun, Xu Wei, and Chen Hongshou, soon followed by Zhu Da, Shitao, Kuncan, and so on.

Alas, this efflorescence of individuality came to an abrupt end with the invasion of the Manchus, whose onslaught the Ming regime, riddled by corruption and riven by internal revolt and rebellion, was in no condition to resist.

I was grateful to the scholar for having drawn my attention back to this period in my country's history. The Ming was significant in and of itself. It also provided a cogent reminder: To evolve, China, like all cultures, needs to enter into dialogue with the best elements of other cultures.

Now I had all I needed to share my reflections about the wealth and amplitude of my native land with colleagues at the conference, and thus already was feeling profoundly thankful

François Cheng

to that scholar and his collection. Then, while looking through a shelf whose contents I had not happened fully to explore, I came upon a book entitled *The Story of the Man of the Mountain*. I don't remember anything particularly eye-catching about its cover. I nonetheless felt immediately drawn to it. A brief preface, handwritten by a contemporary annotator, explained that the work's author was a man of some refinement who had lived toward the end of the Ming period. Following the descent from the north of the Manchus, this individual had refused to serve the new conquerors. Such was not unusual. A number of Ming intellectuals became farmers under the Manchus; others, having taken refuge in remote mountain retreats, devoted their lives to writing as a means of preserving their thoughts and their memories.

The Story of the Man of the Mountain was a love story involving two extraordinary people. The writer learned their tale from someone who had apparently been close to them both. In the story he appears with the name Gan-er.

I began reading the book and from the very first pages was plunged into Ming culture. My state of receptivity heightened by my surroundings, I fell under the story's spell; for quite some time I was incapable of reading anything else and, once I had finished, of thinking about anything else. So taken was I by this book that I decided at one point to extend my stay at the abbey for further study and reflection. In the end, alas, I didn't.

Years passed. I never forgot about that book I had read so passionately; the mere thought of it brought a sharp stab of regret and longing. Then I had occasion to go back to the abbey. Of course I was anxious to locate *The Story of the Man of the Mountain,* to see whether I could recapture the spell it had cast over me. To my stunned surprise—then to my despair—I learned it had disappeared. Clearly I had not been the only one unable to resist its power. Whose hands were holding it now? I somehow knew I would never find it again.

I resolved to reconstitute the story from memory—I had read it many times, and the details remained embroidered upon my mind. For a period of time, circumstances kept me from fulfilling my vow. Now, at last, I am putting pen to paper, hoping that I can capture even a fraction of what had so deeply touched me years before. Whether or not I can, I must try, yielding to its power, however distant its source.

A few words of introduction. Some might feel surprised that the author of this tale, the so-called man of the mountain himself, witness to a period of tremendous artistic and intellectual ferment and of the upheaval brought on by the collapse of a dynasty, decided to tell a love story. I am not surprised. To evoke as well as to escape the turmoil of his times, he had chosen a timeless subject. Romantic love involves far more than the heart and senses, but the spirit. The greatest passions take root not only in the most repressive social settings but during periods when they find a fertile subsoil of heightened spiritual search and self-examination. Conditions at the close of the Ming Dynasty were perfect. By idealizing their feelings for one another tapping into a nearly mystical power, the lovers in the tale engage in a process of continual transcendence.

There is another aspect to this story worthy of mention here. *The Story of the Man of the Mountain* contains the account of a meeting between our protagonist and a "religious stranger" from the "Ocean of the West." Given the historical period under consideration here, this must refer to one of the first Jesuits to have crossed into China. Records indicate that once they had become established, in Beijing particularly, these Jesuits engaged in high-level and very lively discussions with philosophers and intellectuals. Some apparently were influenced by Confucianism's basic tenets, for example, touching upon the dignity of man (who, after Heaven and Earth, represents the third element) or the virtues that inspire our very noblest impulses. These Westerners also converted some of China's greatest scholars and a significant number of other people to Christianity, including members of the ruling family.

This is not the place for discussion of that topic, even less so for a debate about the nature of conversion. The religious stranger in question—almost certainly, as I've suggested, a Jesuit missionary—was making his way to the capital when he and the story's protagonist cross paths. Their meeting therefore happens by merest accident. Nonetheless, the account of it remains both valuable and fascinating. There is an awkward, naïve quality to their conversations, initially characterized by perplexity. Given that these men come from places so distant from each other, it would have taken them time to find common ground. They listen to each other but do not, at first, hear. Partly this is a matter of language. When their discussions touch upon the nature of love, however, something changes. At the moment he meets the religious stranger, you see, our hero is deeply in love, and suffering from the cruel reality of his lover's inaccessibility. He therefore interprets in his own way what the stranger has to say about love.

In the end, a true meeting of spirits always occurs at a level, whether higher or deeper, with a view to the infinite; that level is one upon which a woman and a man might dwell. A look or a smile—surpassing language—are enough to reveal the mystery of the other, and a mystery beyond all other.

François Cheng

永

One

THAT MORNING, AS HE HAD FORESEEN, DAO-SHENG STARTED down the mountain.

The sun had already reached the tops of the trees. Normally he would have departed much earlier—at the monastery everyone rose at cock's crow—but he had had several duties to perform first. After breakfast he had gone to the well to fetch water and brought back several bucketfuls, which he emptied into the enormous urn outside the kitchen. Then he had cut some wood at the edge of the vegetable garden, taking care afterward to find a dry place to store it. Finally, he had taken part in the morning prayers with the Taoist monks. There were fewer of these venerable men than there used to be—seven in all, five of them quite elderly. Dao-sheng had done all this to help out, of course, but also from a strong feeling of gratitude. During the course of his life, he had lived in two Taoist monasteries, though without actually ever taking the vows of a monk; he had therefore not yet arrived at the state of *wu-qing,* total detachment.

This time he was departing without knowing when he would be coming back, or even whether he would be coming back. Asked by one of the monks about this last point, he had remained silent. All that he had said was that he wished to spend a little time near the district capital in the region called South of the River. He had been there as a young man and felt an urge to see it again. The desire to revisit a place from one's past was easily understood by all. Yet the monks would sorely miss Dao-sheng. During the three years he had lived in this particular monastery, he had become greatly valued for his skills in the healing arts. The elderly monks had found him of great solace. So had the pilgrims who came up to the monastery on palanquins, seeking his medical advice. Indeed, the Taoists couldn't help feeling a sense of abandonment at Dao-sheng's leaving; they secretly wished his absence would not be a long one.

Ordinarily, like the monks, Dao-sheng wore a long robe. For his journey down the mountain he had dressed in a simple tunic and trousers. Around his waist was a wide cloth belt, inside of which he had sewn a purse and from which hung a bowl. Walking long distances didn't faze him. On the contrary, he was used to it. It was what he had done in life. He knew to take only the minimum: Extra clothes, a few tools, acupuncture needles, medicinal herbs, and his divination books—rolled up in a cotton blanket that was itself wrapped inside a waterproof oilcloth. The bundle was somewhat bulky, yet how weightless it had seemed to Dao-sheng once hoisted on his back. After taking his leave of the monks, offering to each the same ceremonial gesture of farewell, he had placed his straw hat on his head, taken up his long walking stick, and set off.

It was the middle of the year's third month. On the mountaintop the fog was still dense; cold seeped into the body. Dao-sheng walked carefully across the wild grasses that had overgrown the path. He was glad he had decided to wear his straw sandals. With their thick, absorbent soles, his cloth shoes would already have been soaked and therefore quite useless. His socks were wet but would dry in his sandals once the sun emerged. Relatively few people had climbed up to the monastery during the winter months, and spring had just arrived, so the path was cluttered with hens' nests and scree deposited by runoff. Dao-sheng was unperturbed. He was exhilarated to be on his way, moving limbs numbed by a sedentary life. Joy surged up. He had to force himself to walk slowly. Nature seemed to be responding buoyantly to his every step. Suddenly a hare dashed across the path directly in front of him. Instinctively he raised his walking stick to strike it, then caught himself.

"Why, you're as rambunctious as I am! Great Master always said I had a long way to go to become a priest."

He paused, then spoke again, chastening himself as the Great Master might have. "Now listen. This journey won't be like the others. At all costs you must behave like a *zhen-ren*, a righteous man. Your only hope of reaching Heaven is with a true heart."

Halfway down the mountain Dao-sheng stopped, though he was not yet tired. According to his calculations, he had plenty of time to reach Jie-shi, a town located a reasonable distance from the foot of the mountain, before evening, so there was no need for hurry. A little farther down the path, beneath a towering pine tree, was an enormous flat and square rock outcrop.

From it, one could gaze at the entire valley stretching out below.

The fog had lifted. In the distance were tiny houses, clustering here and there to form villages. Off to one side, along the horizon, rose tall plumes of smoke, indicating the presence of a city and its surrounding towns. There was his ultimate destination. Reaching the source of the smoke would take about two days. Dao-sheng was fairly certain he would arrive there on the fourth day at the very latest.

Midday came and went. The sun grew generous. Crows flapped and rustled among the new foliage filtering the light. Far overhead, a pair of eagles traced invisible circles. It struck Dao-sheng how alive a man in his fifty-fourth year could feel. One more journey did not intimidate him, though he sensed, again, that it might well be his last. Was she still alive? He made a gesture of impatience, as if to swat away insects encircling him—or to dismiss a troublesome thought. He hoisted the bundle onto his back and continued on his way.

As it approached the foot of the mountain, the path grew less steep. The weather was more temperate on this southern side. Terraced rice paddies started appearing, and next to them were fields of corn, soybean, and sugarcane. Ahead of him Dao-sheng could see tea fields. Gradually, houses sprang up, and round them were dense groves of bamboo and well-tended border gardens, and raised beds in which plump vegetables with emerald skins gleamed with reflected sunlight.

How typical all this was of the Jiang-nan, the South of the River region Dao-sheng had known as a youth, when he had been a musician with a traveling theater group. In those days they had moved constantly in covered wagons from one place to the next, affording little chance to admire the landscape. He had never returned. Once, three years before, he had crossed the river from the regions of the North but had almost immediately ascended the northern slope of the valley and climbed up Mount Gan. There he had remained until now.

The river valley's heady charms could not be denied. On the mountaintop one breathed in the scent of moist, moss-covered rocks and ancient trees. Here the air was sweet with the perfume of flowers and fruits, mixed with the smell of strong wine. Intoxication spread through Dao-sheng's limbs.

Two palanquins approached from the opposite direction. Dao-sheng was preparing to move to let them pass by when from out of the first palanquin came a man's voice.

"Are you not the doctor from up above?"

When Dao-sheng acknowledged that he was, the man ordered his porters to stop, then jumped out. Hurriedly explaining that he had been taking his sick wife up to the monastery to seek help, the man got down on his knees and begged Dao-sheng to examine her right away. The wife was in the second palanquin, which Dao-sheng asked be put down on the side of the road. He peered in and saw immediately that the man's wife was indeed very ill, though she was still able to speak. After she described her symptoms, he examined her tongue, pulled back her eyelids and looked into her eyes, and took her pulse. He concluded she had fallen victim to typhoid fever, a serious illness that required urgent care, which was impossible to administer in the present circumstances. He opened his bundle and took out his finest medications, while informing the husband what other plants would need to be added to them, as well as what proportions would be necessary for preparing the final medication. It was, Dao-sheng assured the husband, all that he could do for her. His wife's fate would depend upon the dictates of Heaven.

The husband was deeply grateful to Dao-sheng and wanted to pay him with gold. This Dao-sheng refused, explaining that because he was not a certified doctor he would accept no money unless the person he had treated recovered. The husband tried to insist, but Dao-sheng would not yield. "If she recovers, send payment to the Taoist monastery in the town of Bai-he. You will find it just south of the district capital."

Once on his way again, Dao-sheng pushed himself a little harder than before; he wanted no more unforeseen delays. News of a doctor's presence spread quickly. If he lingered, others would come seeking him out. Apart from the practice of medicine, Dao-sheng's chief profession was divination, whose guiding precept was "Do what you can and leave the rest to Heaven." Indeed, once conditions and opportunities are united, and man has understood what is and what is not within his power, that which must not happen will not happen, and that which must, will.

Before long Dao-sheng had reached the floodplain and joined the ranks of other travelers walking the dusty main road. It was deeply rutted in places but also much wider than the path down the mountain. At the entrance to one of the villages, beneath a giant pagoda, was a stand at which tea and food were sold. Dao-sheng requested some chrysanthemum tea, for he knew it the most thirst-quenching, then drank it in little sips while chewing on peanuts. Suddenly very hungry, he devoured a few sesame pancakes.

Refreshed, Dao-sheng undertook the final leg of the day's journey. He was still walking parallel to the river. The valley grew wider, pushing the surrounding hills further and further apart. He was experiencing that double sensation all wanderers know: The thrill of absolute freedom, on the one hand, and, on the other, the knowledge that you will have to make decisions, such as which path to take or where to spend the night. The sun was beginning to touch the line of hills. To reach the town of Jie-shi before dark, Dao-sheng would have to hurry.

By the time he made it to Jie-shi, the shops had already turned over their lanterns, indicating they were closing. He headed toward the end of the main avenue, next to the bridge, where an old tavern and inn had once been located. It was there. In fact, everything seemed as it had thirty years before— the same sound of the nearby river, the same slightly crooked façade. He knocked at the door. A middle-aged woman opened to him; behind her stood a man, her husband, and apparently the proprietor. Dao-sheng apologized for arriving so late. He explained that though he might have found some other place to spend the night, he had been in search of this particular inn. Thirty or so years before, you see, he had come here as part of a traveling theater troupe. The proprietor's eyes lit up. Though young at the time, he replied, he remembered that troupe very clearly. With one voice, the husband and wife warmly invited Dao-sheng to enter.

The kitchen fire had gone out, so the couple was very concerned to learn their guest had not yet eaten, for they had nothing to offer. Then, an outline of a smile came to the woman's face. She remembered that a caldron of Beef with Five Perfumes had been simmering on the fire all evening long and was probably still hot. The dish had been prepared for a wedding that would take place the next day, but they could easily use a small portion of it as dinner for their unexpected visitor.

Soon Dao-sheng was seated at a table and presented with a large bowl from which emanated a most appetizing smell, as well as a plate of *pao-cai*, marinated vegetables, and a pitcher of wine. Dao-sheng said nothing of being Taoist—or nearly so. Taoists observe strict vegetarianism. Before such warmhearted hosts and such a generous feast, he could not resist. He hungrily devoured the contents of the bowl and drank the entire pitcher of wine.

This first day of my journey has gone well. This is a good sign, he thought, feeling pleasantly tipsy. At the very least, his fear of what he could not foresee was eased.

Two

AFTER THREE DAYS ON THE ROAD, DAO-SHENG ENTERED THE district capital. It was midday. He was hungry as well as tired, but rather than eat he went straight to the *ya-men*, the regional government office and police station, located in the main square. He noted that the once imposing-looking building seemed to have deteriorated somewhat. The paint on the sign and pillars was peeling; they had lost a little of their awe-inspiring authority. Nonetheless, Dao-sheng did not want to sit directly in front of this building. He crouched further off, though choosing a spot from which he could see it. People milled around him. From time to time he was jostled by passersby; sometimes they nearly knocked him over. He took no notice. Compared with what he had been through in his life, this was nothing.

Thirty years before, he had been at this same place, and he had departed from it seated in a cart, his feet chained, his body bound to those of other prisoners by thick rope. Thus had begun the grindingly miserable life of a slave laborer. He remembered that no one in the cart had said a word. Nor did the prisoners dare ask where they were being taken. It made no difference. All they knew was that they were heading to the regions of the North. First they would be taken to the provinces of Luoyang and Kaifeng to help rebuild the fortifications; then they would work on the dikes built along the entire length of the Yellow River.

The grimness of the laborers' lives was beyond description. They lived in flimsy shelters, and the numbers of those who perished were beyond counting. Some were taken by the winter ice and snow, others by epidemics during the torrid summer heat. Then there were those poor souls swept off by floods when the dikes gave way. Had he not made his escape during a rescue attempt, he, Dao-sheng, would have left his white bones to bleach in the red clay along with all the others.

After seven years of servitude, he had become a fugitive, and wandered everywhere. The hard labor had deformed his fingers and left him with a stiff wrist. No longer able to play the violin, he survived by doing menial jobs, sometimes of a criminal nature. Twice he had nearly been recaptured. When he arrived in An-hui, near the city of Xuan-cheng, he decided out of desperation to seek shelter in a monastery on Mount Huang. The Great Master took pity on him and took him in. There he was given the name he now used.

Dao-sheng had served the Great Master with unswerving devotion. There were other disciples. One, named Yun-xian, was acknowledged as the most gifted. He was to have been taught all that the master knew. However, Yun-xian died young. Noting Dao-sheng's quick mind, and despite the fact that the young man showed no particular inclination for monastic life, the Great Master decided to teach Dao-sheng the arts of medicine and divination, so that the secret formulas he knew would not be lost to history.

Dao-sheng stayed in the monastery until the Great Master's death, a total of thirteen years. When he descended Mount Huang, he at least no longer feared starving to death. He went from monastery to monastery. With his knowledge and skill, Dao-sheng found that he could come and go almost as he pleased. Sick people were everywhere. And nearly everyone wondered what the future held for them. Ten years flowed by. Dao-sheng grew heavier, his face became etched with lines, his hair turned gray.

Thus was a life lived. And yet he sometimes wondered, had this been a life? Had he truly lived his life when throughout its length one memory had hung suspended beyond his reach? It always reappeared just when he thought it gone forever. One event had gripped him from the inside and never let go. Sometimes when he thought about it, he couldn't tell whether it had happened or been a dream.

Of course it had happened. Why else would he have been banished and forced into slave labor? Why else would he have forded rivers and streams to return here, obsessed but by one notion?

Returning to the district capital had been no simple matter. Three years earlier, when he had come down from the North and crossed to the river's southern bank, it had taken two weeks to reach the outskirts. There he had begun to question what he was doing. Why come back? To find out where matters stood? What was the point in that? What was the point of finding out whether she was still alive and living with the Zhao family? What would he do afterward? Settle the score with

Second Young Lord Zhao, now simply Second Lord? Was he even alive? Too much had seemed unforeseeable to Dao-sheng. That was why he had faltered. He whose profession was predicting the future for others was incapable of performing the same service for himself.

He had therefore climbed back up Mount Gan, thinking that finally he might renounce this dream. He found he could not. Despite all the meditations and the exercises in vacuity he forced himself to perform, Dao-sheng could not break free from the idea that held him fast in its grasp. From the mountain's summit, his gaze had been irresistibly drawn toward the bottom of the valley and those giant plumes of smoke. Indeed, precisely because of these meditations, Dao-sheng came to realize that he had been brought into this world to pursue that which obsessed him. The passion in his heart would not be uprooted, and nothing could prevent it from living out its allotted time.

In a shop not far from the *ya-men,* Dao-sheng gulped down a bowl of noodle soup, wiped his mouth, then headed off in the direction of the city's southern gate. Once outside, he walked for a few *li* until he came to the outskirts of Bai-he. This was his destination, a town as busy as the district capital itself. Bai-he had everything—a Taoist monastery, a Buddhist temple, markets, inns; it would be an ideal place in which to practice his professions. He was also aware that the Zhao estate was a mere five *li* away.

In Bai-he, he asked directions to the monastery and wound his way through a maze of alleys and passageways until he

François Cheng

arrived in a peaceful part of town. There he located the monastery, surrounded by shabby-looking dwellings. He pushed open the door, crossed the courtyard, and came upon the *fang-zhang,* the monastery's master. Dao-sheng explained briefly who he was and where he was from. The master led him through the rear courtyard and, at the far end of a long inner passage, showed him into a small room furnished only with a bed and table. Shutters made of small squares covered with paper filtered the light. Situated as it was at the back of the monastery, the room was very quiet. It was exactly what Dao-sheng had hoped for. He proposed to pay rent, while also pledging to take part in the daily chores.

Several days after his arrival, he went to the town's main square to pay his respects to the Great Monk of the Buddhist temple. He found himself in the presence of a tall man with a generous face and penetrating gaze, clearly deserving of his reputation for virtue and wisdom. The temple was very popular. All day long people burned incense or prayed, or came to listen to the litanies sung by the monks. There was plenty of activity outside as well; the commercial streets all around the temple were packed. Dao-sheng asked the Great Monk for permission to set up his consultation stand to the right of the temple's steps, so that he might practice physiognomy and divination. The Great Monk was somewhat perplexed by the request. Dao-sheng explained that, though not a priest, he had spent many years studying divination as well as medicine with a great Taoist master. He was not a certified doctor, but he knew a number of therapeutic remedies and could administer acupuncture. He had often been summoned when the certified doctors had done all they could, and he had success treating malaria, dysentery, typhoid, diseases of the liver and the lymph, arthritis and rheumatism, as well as certain women's ailments. He charged no fee unless the patient recovered.

What Dao-sheng said made excellent sense to the Great Monk, and his sincere and open attitude impressed and moved the holy man. He agreed that Dao-sheng be accorded a short trial period.

At the end of just a month, not only was the Great Monk fully confident in Dao-sheng's abilities but he felt bonds of friendship with him. For several years he had suffered from severe rheumatism; after Dao-sheng's treatments, the Great Monk noted a marked improvement in his condition. Moreover, the husband of the woman with typhoid fever paid an honorarium to the monastery; his wife had recovered. Before leaving, the husband had burned incense in the temple and praised Dao-sheng's skills to the Great Monk. Just as he had on the first night of the journey, Dao-sheng felt that omens seemed favorable. He still did not know, however, whether the goal he had ventured south to attain was real or based upon a dream.

In the meantime, his life assumed a certain routine. Every evening he returned to the monastery and ate dinner with the Taoists. Every morning, after helping the monks with their chores, he went to the Buddhist temple. He searched out his spot near the foot of the steps, set up his stand, and began to offer consultations. At noon he took his lunch at one of the many eateries located nearby.

His stand afforded him an excellent view of the teeming street life, the incessant movement and brilliant colors, the confused din of animals, carts, and shouting that seemed to come from all directions. The air abounded with odors—of wine, spices, every sort of oil, meats, grilled pancakes, and manure. The square in front of the temple was quite spacious. On the far side a large tree-lined avenue extended into the distance. Diagonally across was a place of worship, smaller than the temple. This was dedicated to the Earth gods.

The crowds of faithful who came to light incense in the temple were from every walk of life. In addition to the townsfolk, there were the peasants from the surrounding countryside. From time to time women wearing finery and the occasional dignitary deigned to join the ordinary folk to offer their devotions. Coming, going, pushing, getting out of the way—there was constant agitation yet also general harmoniousness.

The temple's popularity was doubtless related to what was happening in the world outside. The empire of the Mings continued its decline; the numbers of riots and kidnappings were growing, alarmingly. This particular province was among the most prosperous, but after several years of bad crops, civil unrest and criminality were on the rise here as elsewhere. At the moment, because new security forces had been brought in to maintain order, calm had temporarily been restored to the region. Nonetheless, the spirits of men remained uneasy. For these reasons, Dao-sheng had little idle time; divination seemed to offer people some measure of certitude.

The days passed. Dao-sheng got to know the others with whom he shared his turf: the one-armed beggar with the limp; the old woman who walked hunched over; the good-natured barber who made a joke of nearly everything. There was the pregnant woman, carrying a baby under her arm and followed around by another child; she was generous with her theories about deadly childhood diseases. There was the *xiu-cai*, the scholar who had taken, and failed, the degree-qualifying examination eight times, and who always resorted to divination before an examination. The scholar had his own stand, at which he exercised the vocation of public scribe. There was the band of hoodlums who harassed any poor servant girl with the ill fortune to cross their path. Last, there was the fat butcher who ran off to the tavern at every opportunity to get away from his nagging wife.

These people formed their own universe, the lines on their faces and hands unique. Dao-sheng reflected upon how this lower world was a showcase of incredible diversity. No two people were alike. Nor would be their fates—happy fates and unhappy fates, enviable lives and miserable lives. He wondered whether the ideal would be for every face and every fate to be identical. Were that so, how could one be filled with admiration for someone of exceptional virtue, or possessed of peerless beauty? It would be like eating the same meal every day. The greater the differences among people, the more interesting life was. Look at the Persians who came to the city to sell their mirrors and rugs; how different they were, with their swarthy skin, dark eyes, and curly hair. They were as compelling as an enigma. Once, Dao-sheng had also seen two tall men fair of complexion and hair crossing the square. The mystery of their origins exceeded all others.

As for the one for whom Dao-sheng's heart yearned, she was close by now. According to what he had heard, the legitimate first wife of Second Lord Zhao, she who had formerly been a member of the Lu family, was still alive. What her life had been like and what it was like now were yet to be discovered, though

Dao-sheng knew that his inquiries would have to be as discreet as possible. Twice he had gone to the Zhao estate, but the outer walls were too high to peer over and the front gate was always closed. He would learn what he needed to learn little by little.

One day, while the Great Monk was having Dao-sheng apply needles to him, one of the holy man's faithful flock came into the room. He and the Great Monk spoke for a while. As he was taking his leave, the visitor made an observation.

"What a long time it has been," he said, "since the lady from the Zhao household has come to the temple to burn incense."

Three

THE NORMALLY PLACID FACE OF THE GREAT MONK GREW animated on the day Dao-sheng finally ventured to ask him about the Zhao family.

"Ah, well! That is a long story. From the days of its ancestors this family was a great source of local pride. Generation after generation occupied important posts in the capital. With their revenue they bought lands, leasing them to farmers. The family fortune grew to be quite considerable. Then came the generation before this one. Great Lord Zhao managed to reach only the rank of *ju-ren,* the lowest degree. His whole life he worked as a local civil servant, though the family maintained its place on the rolls.

"At present the family estate is divided between his sons, First Lord and Second Lord. Their two holdings are adjacent but divided by a contiguous wall. Each side has its own courts and gardens, and keeps to its own ways. There seems to be peace between them. First Lord tried to pass his examinations, without success. Still, he is a cultivated and sensible man. He bought a title and spent a little time in a provincial city, then came back to devote himself to the family's welfare.

"His return had been necessary, for Second Lord did not prove up to the job of managing the estate. He's a debauched soul, and as tyrannical as they come. He was born that way. Nothing to be done about it. Outside the estate he lived a life of lechery. Inside he does as he pleases. He's cruel to the servants and to the tenant farmers. When these latter are unable to pay the rent, they have to sell their children. His wife ceaselessly counsels goodness and moderation, but her words fall on deaf ears.

"She herself is a saint. What ill luck for her that she ever became part of the Zhao family. People call her Lady Ying because her first name is Lan-ying, 'slender orchid.' She comes from the Lu family, which once was powerful but fell on hard times. When she was pledged to the Zhao family, it was with the idea of giving new luster to her family's reputation. Little did they know what a soulless wretch her intended would turn out to be! After the marriage she suffered miscarriages, then was ill for several years. Second Lord meanwhile took a concubine, Lady Fu-chun. They have a son who's already grown up. I don't know if he turned out well or not, for he hasn't returned from Nanking, where he went looking for work. Later they had another son and a daughter, who I believe are twelve or thirteen.

"Second Lord is decidedly insatiable. He took a second concubine, whose name I have forgotten—a young girl from a peasant family whom he had seduced. Out of the goodness of his heart he decided not to abandon her. He might very well have done just that. There was a *ya-tou*, a servant girl bought by

François Cheng

the family, whom he also took advantage of and then resold. The poor child has ended up in a brothel. The second concubine was never very happy and died a few years later, leaving an orphan boy. And that's the family story."

"I have heard that Lady Ying . . . often visits the temple," said Dao-sheng.

"It is true. Lady Ying was completely shunted aside by her husband and lives alone in the west wing of the house, attended by her servant, Xiao-fang. She has gradually turned toward Buddhism, to the great happiness of our flock. Kind and generous, she practices charity and comes often to the temple to pay her devotions. As you have heard, we have not seen her for some time now. I inquired after her and am told that she is doing poorly. Nonetheless, she continues to give out food to the poor every day at noon at the back gate of the Zhao estate. Her health never recovered from a serious incident that took place some years back."

Though burning with impatience to know what this event might have been, Dao-sheng remained silent.

"I was a witness to it, for I happened to have become involved. To do it justice will take time." The Great Monk had warmed to the subject; nothing would stop him now.

"It was seven or eight years ago. After the harvest the bandits came. Second Lord's portion of the estate is nearest the main road, and so it was there that they attacked, carrying off grain and looting precious objects. This took longer than they had counted on, but before the soldiers arrived they started a fire and beat Second Lord with a heavy stick. Worse, they abducted Lady Ying."

"Oh!"

"Ah yes. These were days of terrible anxiety. We lived in constant fear for Lady Ying's life. After several interminable days without news, Xiao-fang came in secret to tell me that an envoy from the bandits had come to the Zhao estate, seeking an exorbitant ransom. No one would touch Lady Ying if they were paid, he said, and then left. After several days it became clear that the Zhao family was delaying paying the ransom. Perhaps this was because of what had happened to Second Lord. The beating he had received had left him partially paralyzed. Or perhaps they had decided to abandon Lady Ying to her fate. Whatever the case, I took it upon myself to raise the sum from among the congregation and took a chair into the mountains to negotiate with the bandits.

"I managed to find their hideout—a few squalid-looking shacks. It was clear they were ready to decamp at a moment's notice. Once I was brought before their leaders, I could see that I was dealing with savages but also that they had been driven to this crime by misery. They talked quite openly with me, for I was neither from the police nor from the Zhao family. Like them, I lived outside society. I explained that the money I had managed to collect was less than what they had demanded but that more could be gotten when they had need. I gave them my word as head of the temple. My sincerity touched them. They accepted my terms.

"For all that I have renounced the things of this world, and banished forever all bonds of attachment, I confess I wept openly when Lady Ying was led out from behind the shacks. She was terribly thin, her face was emaciated, but her dignified and somber bearing still commanded respect. I was not surprised that the bandits thanked me as they handed her over to my care.

"Darkness was falling, but I decided to descend the mountain that very night. They put Lady Ying into the chair. I followed a few feet behind. It was the sixteenth day of the eighth month. A full moon floated in the sky, making the path glisten. It was a wondrous sight. At first all was silent. Then, as night deepened, I heard the wind rustling the grass, the chirr of insect wings, and the sound of footsteps echoing off the mountainsides. Now and then came the sweet voice of Lady Ying, who from her chair would turn around and say, 'Great Monk, I hope you are not too tired.'

"I was not tired at all. I had brought someone back to life. Heaven and Earth seemed to recognize this. Rescuing Lady Ying was without a doubt the finest thing I have done in this life, thanks be to merciful Buddha."

"Then what happened?" Dao-sheng asked.

"Upon her return, Lady Ying fell sick. As the proverb goes, 'The greater the calamity one has endured, the greater the happiness one can experience.' Her devotion to Buddha grew with each passing day. Our priesthood reveres her. The Zhao family reimbursed us the money we had raised. They explained that at the time they had been overwhelmed by events. Second Lord, as I said, was paralyzed. This has merely worsened his character. He shuts everyone out now, permitting Lady Fu-chun alone to attend to his needs. Lady Ying is left to herself more than before. She visits Second Lord only on special occasions. They use servants as intermediaries when they have matters to discuss. Yet I would say she prefers her new living conditions. She takes advantage of them to come to the temple to burn incense and perform other acts of devotion. She works hard to ease the plight of the poor, and helps whenever she can. To us she has become more than merely precious—she has become . . . irreplaceable."

Four

A SMALL GROUP OF PEOPLE, PERHAPS THIRTY IN ALL, GATHERED at the back gate of the Zhao estate at midday. They were ragged and shoeless, reduced to seeking charity. Among them were women with children. Some stood on the dusty ground; others crouched, each holding a bowl and chopsticks. They jabbered and called out to one another. Today a newcomer crouched nearby with his bowl and sticks. No one paid him any attention.

A moment later came the sound of the heavy bar being lifted. The gate opened with a grinding sound. In silent anticipation everyone waited for the Zhao servants Lao Sun and Zhu the Sixth to put a large covered vat of cooked rice on bricks set directly on the ground. Behind them was the maid Xiao-fang. Small but sturdy, she carried a caldron brimming with steamed vegetables, which she placed on a specially built stand, managing this by herself. Now was the moment for Lady Ying. When she appeared, people converged upon her. There were cries of "Lady of the Kind Heart!" and "Bountiful Lady!" She begged them not to push; there would be enough for everyone. Her words seemed to have no effect on the hungry group. Lao Sun repeated them in a louder voice. "Do not crowd, please! The lady has told you that you will all be served."

He lifted the lid from the vat of rice; steam poured out. He handed the lid to Zhu the Sixth and a ladle to Lady Ying, who skillfully placed a portion of rice and then vegetables into each bowl. Once someone had received his share, he mumbled his thanks and retreated somewhere to eat. Some moved further away, such as to the foot of the willows located on the far side of the road; there they sat and slowly consumed the contents of their bowls. Once their simple meal was finished, they lingered for a moment or two before getting up and shuffling off.

Dao-sheng waited until last. His heart was beating wildly. He could not believe that he was seeing Lan-ying again—alive, here, before his eyes—and was amazed that he could still recognize her. She was forty-eight years old now, but her serene and refined presence was unchanged. Her light blue dress covered her from her feet to the top of her neck, exposing only her silvered hair done up in a bun, her pale hands and cheeks, and her lips with their hint of color. The impression of solemnity she gave was heightened by a sadness that seemed to shadow her. She performed her charity silently and with an air of melancholy.

Finally, Dao-sheng approached, not daring to look at her face. He extended his bowl and waited. At the moment he offered his thanks, he directed his eyes to hers and gazed upon the face that he had carried in his heart for these many years. This brief glimpse was enough. He saw through the paleness, the sadness, the gentle sag around the eyebrows, the slightly puffy cheeks, and found the purity of the lines in her face and

François Cheng

expression in her eyes that long ago had first touched his heart, then broken it.

Dao-sheng went back day after day. He learned to rejoice silently in Lan-ying's presence, for periods that were brief yet indelible. At any moment of the day, the memory of it could make him tremble with happiness even while it made his heart tighten. To others, she was but a kindly woman in middle age. He tried to remember if he had seen her smile. Yes, that time the lame beggar arrived late. He had come hobbling down the road on his crutch, calling out. She had had to scrape the bottom of the rice vat to find anything for his bowl, which he held out with his one free hand. Flustered, he exclaimed in defense of his tardiness, "Well, at least this way you won't have to wash the pan. It's been wiped clean!"

That had brought the smile, as quick as a darting swallow, lighting up her face.

Dao-sheng knew that smile. In the whole of this human world, it was perhaps the only thing that had retained its magic and mystery. What had happened thirty years before came back to him, down to the smallest detail.

Old Lord Lu was celebrating his seventieth birthday. The great room of his estate was lit up by a thousand lanterns. After a banquet, a theater troupe put on a performance. The musical accompaniment was played by musicians seated along the length of a side wall. Dao-sheng, the youngest of them, was at the end of the row, playing his *erhu*. During the moments when he wasn't playing, he had a chance to look around and soon realized that in fact he was being accorded a most privileged view: he need only turn his head slightly to observe the women, who were sequestered behind a screen set near the back wall. The women could hear the music and peek over the screen to catch a glimpse of the show. Dao-sheng couldn't help glancing at them.

Suddenly—yet as if he had expected it—his gaze met that of another. It belonged to a young woman in a red dress. Disconcerted, he almost forgot to pick up his violin to play. When he had the chance to look at the screen again, he was overjoyed to see that the young woman continued to look at him; she smiled, an act of unbelievable candor. The lanterns and the candles seemed to dim; the only light came from the intersection of their gazes. It was Lan-ying, of the Lu family. He had met her three years earlier, when his troupe had played in a neighboring village. They had exchanged glances then as well.

So it is her! he thought. It is almost as if we had arranged this. A young woman in full flower—an orchid, or a lotus with red petals. Is this pure chance? Does fate have something to do with this?

Dao-sheng told himself to stop daydreaming. He was but a poor musician.

In the time that it took Dao-sheng to emerge from his reverie, she had vanished, and in her place were two other young women, one dressed in green and the other in yellow, both with braided hair. Servants, apparently. A moment later, these were replaced by a middle-aged woman wearing a dress with garnet brocade. Her noble demeanor denoted that she was the mistress of the house. Dao-sheng regretted bitterly that he had not responded to Lan-ying's smile with one of his own. He might never get the opportunity again.

After the lady in the garnet brocade came older women, grandparents or servants, poking their noses over the screen. Sadly and a little distractedly, Dao-sheng forced himself to focus on his *erhu,* particularly since his neighbor, an older musician, had jabbed him with his elbow to get him back in line. While he played, Dao-sheng stared ahead vacantly. Then something red caught his eye. He turned his head and saw her. He thought he might be dreaming. In the unreal atmosphere produced by the candles and colored lanterns and actors in bright costumes, everything vacillated between reality and illusion. He fought his anxiety, repeating over and over to himself, "Don't miss this chance!"

But was it her?

It was. The luminous face, the living, breathing, graceful outline, the hair done up in a bun, setting off the red of her dress. She was a gift from Heaven. Dao-sheng's profound sense of recognition dissolved his shyness. In this precious interval between Sky and Earth, without other witnesses, they were together. She smiled, no longer simply in a candid way but with greater meaning. He smiled back. He bobbed his head to the rhythm of the music as a sign of assent, and she seemed to do the same. He lost track of where he was. He was floating in a separate sphere. How long this lasted he could not tell. He was still floating in it when once again he sought out Lan-ying's gaze, but his misted eyes prevented him from seeing her clearly. He calmly allowed himself to become enveloped in the sweet light emanating from this face, so close and so far away. What came to him was the image of a petal falling to earth. At that very instant, the clash of the cymbals and tambourines announced that the show had ended.

The spectators rose to their feet, some shouting, *Hao! Hao!* One last time Dao-sheng looked toward the screen; there was no one. Only a small bright spot on the ground. He took advantage of the general commotion to approach the screen and pick up the object. It was a handkerchief.

Among the spectators that same evening was Second Young Lord of the Zhao family. The insolence of the musician who instead of humbly doing his job dared to ogle the women had not escaped his notice. It didn't take much imagination to realize that among the women there was one whom this ruffian had most hoped to spy upon. That young woman was none other than his betrothed, Lan-ying.

After the birthday celebration, Second Young Lord and some of his friends went to the large inn at the Southern Gate of the capital, where the troupe was spending the night. They ordered wine and food. After a jolly evening, Second Young Lord asked the proprietor to bring the troupe's leader to him. When the leader appeared, Second Young Lord told him that he wished to hear the young violinist play something. No one contested the power of the Zhao family. Even the regional administrators scraped and bowed to them. Despite the lateness of the hour, the leader found Dao-sheng and ordered him to play for these distinguished clients. Dao-sheng played a short piece, thinking that would satisfy them; to his great surprise, it was received not with praise but with insults. He played a second piece as conscientiously as he could. Again his listeners made fun of him. They asked how someone with such a tin ear could be part of a musical troupe. Now Dao-sheng realized that these men were trying to rattle him; they meant him harm. When they asked him to play a third piece, he refused.

"Why, given that you think I have no talent?"

"Never two without three!" insisted Second Young Lord. "I'm only asking you to play again to see if there's any hope for you at all." He winked at his companions, who burst out laughing.

Dao-sheng pressed his violin under his arm. "I said no and I meant it."

His adversary banged his fist on the table. "Second Young Lord Zhao asks you to play and you dare to refuse him?"

Dao-sheng suddenly realized what was behind all this. Second Young Lord had seen him looking behind the screen during the performance. Yet he remained sure there was no way anyone could have seen him exchange looks with Lan-ying.

But Second Young Lord rose to his feet, advancing toward Dao-sheng. "What kind of dog are you to think you had the right to look at the women straight in the eyes?" he hissed.

And with that Second Young Lord prepared to strike the object of his fury. Dao-sheng pushed him away with all his might. His assailant fell backward, knocking over the table behind him. Second Young Lord jumped up and ran at Dao-sheng with a knife. His back to the wall, Dao-sheng grabbed a stool and waved it in the air, unintentionally hitting Second Young Lord in the arm and one of his friends in the chin. There was blood. Someone—a crony of Second Young Lord—called for the fight to stop and ordered that Dao-sheng be subdued. Dao-sheng was tied up and placed under guard while the wounded men were treated and then went home to bed.

Although he had acted in self-defense, Dao-sheng was brought before the city tribunal. He pleaded his innocence, but the cause was lost. Second Young Lord and his friend testified that Dao-sheng had attacked them. After several days in prison, he was condemned to banishment and forced labor. In prison another condemned man told him he was lucky; banishment was better than the stick treatment, which could leave you maimed for life.

As an orphan, Dao-sheng had been sold to a theater troupe. Life on the road hadn't always been easy. All year long they had roamed from village to village, door to door. Sometimes they had been chased off, and often they didn't have enough to eat. Still, they had had one another. And Dao-sheng had loved playing the violin; everyone agreed that he was gifted. Had Lan-ying smiled at him because of his appearance (people said he was very handsome) or because of the beauty of his playing? Both perhaps. He couldn't bear the thought that he would never see her again.

The innocent young woman, so pure of the dust and smoke of this world, would never learn what Second Young Lord had done, or what Dao-sheng was now about to endure.

François Cheng

Five

DAO-SHENG WENT TO THE BACK GATE OF THE ZHAO ESTATE each day at noon. He was rewarded with the vision of that face whose traces of sadness made it all the more precious to him. What he felt when he saw it would not be described. The rest of that day he spent waiting anxiously for the next, eased somewhat by the assurance that she would be there. She always was. It was as if they had planned a lovers' rendezvous, though he knew that she could have no idea of who he was. Perhaps, one day she would appear because of him. A self-centered thought, and an unimaginable one. Taoist philosophy had taught Dao-sheng not to desire too much. Still, that he could see her, unaware as she was of what this meant to him, offered one of the few feelings of happiness that he had ever known.

When Lan-ying appeared one day at the beginning of winter, he could tell from her face that she had become more ill. Advancing toward her to receive his portion, he peered closely at the dark circles around her eyes. His uneasiness grew. He began to have an ominous feeling.

After Lao Sun and Zhu the Sixth had carried off the vat and the caldron, Lady Ying and Xiao-fang returned to their wing of the Zhao estate, following the path that went through the garden. Passing next to its man-made hill, they heard the wailing of a child. They came around the side of the hill, and there they found Gan-er, the orphan left by Second Lord's second concubine. He was curled up in the weeds, and his entire body was trembling. Lifting his head, they saw that his forehead was cut and his cheeks had scratch marks; he was bleeding from the nose. When they asked who had done these things to him, he at first refused to reply. Eventually they got him to mention Zhu-er and Ju-er, the son and daughter of Lady Fu-Chun, as well as the children living in the house of First Lord. They did not behave like a brother and sister to Gan-er. They picked on the young boy.

"They wanted me to be a dog and roll over, and then a monkey climbing in the trees. I didn't want to, and so they beat me and I fought back. They pinned me on the ground and I bit their hands. Ju-er squeezed my throat and I pulled her hair. They started hitting me and wouldn't stop, and then left me there. I haven't dared to move."

Lady Ying took Gan-er to her room. She cleaned him off and let him lie on her bed. Turning toward Xiao-fang, she said in a low voice, speaking more to herself than to her servant, "I am at fault with regard to the second concubine. Before she died she asked me to protect her son, and Gan-er lived with me for several years. When I was kidnapped by the bandits, the child was placed in the care of Lady Fu-chun. When I returned, I became sick and could do little. Fu-chun continued to care for the boy. This was the wish of Second Lord. I did not want to go against his wishes, and so things remained. The children are all growing up, and I thought they had become better behaved. Gan-er is a quiet child and never lets on when he is unhappy. Today I see that I must take him back. That will displease Second Lord and Fu-chun."

With a sigh, she added, "And if something happens to me, this child will be even more unhappy."

Xiao-fang reflected on her mistress's words for a moment, then replied in a decisive voice. "We will take him back. I will see to it. But you must not say 'If something happens to me.' Nothing will happen to you. I am here to take care of you, and you will continue to live. The matter is simple. I will not leave you. As long as you are here, I will be here. Anyway, should anything happen, I will take Gan-er far away."

"Listen to you! A woman cannot go very far, not unless she gets married."

"I don't plan to get married."

"Without a husband you can go no further than a convent."

"So I'll go to the convent. And Gan-er will become a bonze and live with the other monks in the temple. That will be better than staying here!"

Xiao-fang's candor brought a smile to Lady Ying's lips. But it faded when she felt her head begin to spin. Seeing that something was wrong, Xiao-fang asked Gan-er to get up and help her get their mistress to bed.

At that same moment, Zhu-er and Ju-er ran into Lady Fu-chun's chambers. As soon as they saw their mother, the brother and sister began to babble their version of what happened.

"Look what Gan-er did to me! He bit my hand!"

"And he pulled my hair!"

"That little thug deserves another slap. No dinner for him this evening! Now go get yourselves cleaned up by Jiao-ma. I am going to give your father his back treatment."

So saying, she went into the chamber next door to give Second Lord a *chui-bei*, gently beating him on the back to relax the muscles. The air in the spacious room was heavy with the odor of opium; the windows that faced the garden were closed because of the cold. Fu-chun went straight to the bed where Second Lord lay under thick spreads. She helped him sit up and started the treatment.

"Does that feel better?"

Second Lord made no reply. "Umm, umm. Ahh, ahh," he moaned.

"Gan-er is becoming more and more insolent. I raised him as best I could, but he's ungrateful."

"He's a good-for-nothing. Forget about him."

"By the way, in First Lord's quarters everyone has gotten new quilted vests. Yet he says that the harvest was not good this year and that he will be forced to cut back on our expenses."

Second Lord coughed deeply and lengthily before responding. "Don't go looking for trouble. My brother is in charge now, and we must accept his authority. He's fair, on the whole. The family isn't what it once was. At least we have everything we need."

The old servant Jiao-ma appeared. She informed them that Xiao-fang had come to say that Lady Ying was ill, and that Lao Sun had been sent to fetch the doctor, Master Wang.

"Thank you for informing us," replied Fu-chun in Second Lord's place.

"Lady Ying doesn't look well," he said. "The other day, when it was milder and you put me near the window, I saw her from afar, crossing the garden along the path. She walked slowly. Her face was as white as paper. I would guess she's not much better off than I am. Neither of us is long for this world."

"Why must Second Lord talk in this way? Why compare yourself to Lady Ying? She is sad all the time and there's nothing anyone can do about it. You know the things I do for you. Despite what you have suffered, you will live a good long time. You yourself said that First Lord was now in charge. So you have nothing to worry about. Here everything follows your every wish. When you want me to be with you, I am with you. When you want to sleep alone because of your coughing or your pains, I leave you alone. When I go to the town to shop, Jiao-ma brings your tea and lights your pipe and tends the fire. Lao Sun lends a hand when you desire to be moved. All of your needs are seen to."

"All that is true, I cannot deny it," replied Second Lord. "What must happen to Lady Ying will happen. Heaven works in its own ways. To tell you the truth, I have not cared for a long time if something should befall her. It will be one worry less. You would rest easier as well."

His words touched Fu-chun very deeply, but she concealed this in a tone of false sincerity. "I have never believed that. Let us simply say that while she is sick she will stop giving away food at the back gate. This will save us all a little money."

"I have thought the same thing, though I cannot forbid her from doing it because of the Great Monk and because at stake here is the family's reputation, which suffered when we were slow in paying Lady Ying's ransom. We have had to pay twice as much attention to it as before."

François Cheng

Six

ONE FULL MONTH, THOUGHT DAO-SHENG. ONE FULL MONTH without seeing you, Lan-ying. Day after day I have waited. You are getting sicker. Would you simply leave this world without a word?

Since my return I have seen you many dozens of times, each so brief and yet long enough to be the happiest moments of my life, for they proved that you were no dream but flesh and blood. You seemed melancholy, but with time I knew that your former beauty would come back. The years have changed the body, not the heart. The heart might be sealed up, but like a piece of jade it glows even in the darkest shadows. Otherwise it could not have created that face and that smile, that look which once seen is never forgotten. Your face has followed me my whole life. Even when I believed it was gone forever, it shone in some secret part of my body.

I rejoiced at merely seeing you, not at the privilege of exchanging looks with you. I stared at you, but you did not see me, much less observe me. Will you recognize me after thirty years of wandering? On the surface I have become this weather-beaten and stiff old man, so different from the lithe young musician of long ago. Look beyond that and you will find the same flame burns within. The spirit that gives it life did not change. Can you still see it?

A month passed, then a second month. Dao-sheng could endure no more. When he had wandered the world, he had been able to overcome all obstacles. Three years before, when he had crossed the river and returned, he had been equally full of hope and then lost it. Now, again, he felt he was losing it. The anxiety was beyond bearing, even more so the feeling of powerlessness. This sharpened his desire to act. If he didn't he would regret it for the rest of his life. But do what? Send a message to the Zhao family and propose to take care of Lady Ying? What could he do that the finest doctors in the city could not?

He found it difficult to focus on what his clients told him. Dao-sheng saw very clearly that in this lower world the affairs of humans revolved around basic themes: birth, love, illness, death; in between might be a pinch of aspiration here, a dash of passion over there, their variation depending on the place, time, and person involved. Take love, for example. For some it was a matter of vanity. For others it meant pledging yourself for eternity. Some changed partners like clothes; others waited their entire lives for one true love.

Thus it was with other things as well. Every client seemed to repeat more or less the same questions: Will this trip go well? What day would be best for opening the shop? When will my wife become pregnant? When will my husband return home? Will I be promoted? Will my luck hold? Will I live a long time? And yet everyone reacted differently to Dao-sheng's predictions. Some were cheerful and self-assured. Most were uncertain or resigned.

Perhaps one should simply limit oneself to being aware of the variety of human signs and assign the same value to everything. Because of his own torments and doubts, Dao-sheng's thoughts went beyond this. One day he remembered the Great Master, who taught him that divination and medicine were merely concoctions. They are nothing without the thought behind them. That is what must be remembered at the hour of greatest despair. Everything is connected. Human signs are inseparable from those of Earth and Sky. What connects them in the heart of this undivided whole is not chain or rope but the breath that both unifies and guarantees a constant process of transformation.

How central is that breath. Combining with the living breaths that are the Yin, the Yang, and the Space Between, the so-called Middle Void, the Primordial Breath created the Heavens, the Earth, and the Ten Thousand Beings. Once the living universe was constituted, the living breaths continued to work, of course. Otherwise the universe would not hold together. That's exactly the point. Disorder and chaos prove these breaths are not alike. Some are destructive, pernicious, and wicked. Hence the notion of the *shen,* spirit breath, divine breath, the basis of all that is true and just. The *shen* is the highest form of living breaths. Ensuring that the great rhythm of the Tao will continue uninterrupted, it ensures at the same time the infallible principle, according to which "Life gives birth to life," in the key phrase of the *I Ching,* the *Book of*

Changes. The *shen* does not predetermine fate. Nevertheless, only those signs produced by the *shen*, and guided by it, are valid. The work of a soothsayer or a doctor consists precisely of capturing the *shen* that exists within the human body as much as it does within the universe, for the body is more than flesh and blood. It is a condensation of breaths. To the degree that any soothsayer or doctor can capture a living entity's *shen*, he can set it back on the path of life.

Tossed about by the events around him, Dao-sheng had begun to forget all this, so it returned with the power of a new revelation, and was an unexpected source of help. He thought of Lan-ying, and of himself, and became convinced that their fates were linked not merely by emotions but by the *shen*. Given the strangeness of the situations into which life had put them, Dao-sheng knew he had to rely on the *shen*—to live, to act, and to guide them to what was true and just.

That same day, during a consultation, Dao-sheng lifted his head and happened to see a woman climb the temple steps. She was sturdy-looking and resolute, but this could not disguise the expression of concern on her face. It was Xiao-fang. He whispered a quick word to his client, rose from his place, and hurried inside the temple. Making his way through the crowd, Dao-sheng found Xiao-fang kneeling in a corner, lighting incense and bowing deeply. After several minutes, she got up and prepared to leave.

Dao-sheng stood before her. "Please pardon me for disturbing you. Two months ago I went to get food at the back gate of the Zhao estate and . . ."

Xiao-fang glanced at him, vaguely recognizing who he was.

"How is Lady Ying?" he blurted out.

"She isn't getting better. We don't know what will happen."

"I am a doctor. I might be able to help."

"She is being cared for by Master Wang and Master Liu. They seem able to do little. . . . Please excuse me. I must hurry home. My mistress will need me."

Dao-sheng felt as if struck on the head with a stick. The pain stirred what vital breath remained within him. He walked straight toward the Great Monk's prayer room, which was in the temple's inner courtyard, behind the large common room. The holy man was sitting on his cushion in the lotus position.

"Lady Ying of the Zhao family is gravely ill. There is no time to lose. Permit me to do something."

Preoccupied though he was, the Great Monk replied. "I fear that Second Lord would not grant permission. He has complete confidence in Master Liu and in Master Wang, whereas about you he knows nothing."

Then he added, "However, one would regret not doing something. We would be doing Lady Ying an injustice. As you say, there is no time to lose. So I will go."

The guardian at the gate of the Zhao estate informed the servant Lao Sun; Lao Sun informed Jiao-ma, the elderly maidservant; Jiao-ma informed Lady Fu-chun, the concubine; and Fu-Chun informed Second Lord. Eventually, the Great Monk was permitted to enter the room. It was redolent of opium smoke.

"Second Lord feels well?"

"I suffer from a great many things. However, what can one do but accept matters? For the moment I have nothing in particular to complain about."

"Lady Ying has not come to the temple for some time. I have learned that she is ill and am filled with concern."

"She has been treated first by Master Liu and then by Master Wang. All that it is humanly possible to do has been done. Now we must trust in the will of Heaven."

"Permit me to hope you will consider a request. Not long ago, a Taoist doctor moved to our town. He has a stand next to the temple where he practices divination, but he also has skills to treat sickness. He does not pretend he can cure everything, but he possesses remedies that have proven effective. I myself have benefited from them."

"You are talking about a healer. I have seen my share come through here, you know. They're all charlatans!"

Nonetheless, given the supplicating look on the face of the Great Monk, Second Lord was hesitant to give a categorical refusal. "I will consider your request and convey to you my response."

The Great Monk saw that pushing the matter further served no purpose and so took his leave.

Lady Fu-chun entered Second Lord's chamber. "That monk seems to have nothing better to do than irritate us."

"I fear we cannot refuse his request. For the same reason as usual—that we must be mindful of what people will say. They'll accuse us of not having done our duty. He wants us to try out his healer. Very well. We'll give in to his wishes. In any case, it will be for the last time."

Seven

.

THE DREAM THAT DAO-SHENG HAD CARRIED FOR SO LONG WAS
becoming true. Guided by Lao Sun, he crossed the threshold of
the Zhao estate and entered the main courtyard, then walked
along a passageway that ran the length of the great room and
led to an inner courtyard. In the middle stood four ancient
pine trees surrounded by worn stone benches. No one was
about at this hour. A flock of sparrows pecked in the dirt,
chirping loudly.

They left the courtyard, crossed though a large room, furnished but not occupied, and went down a narrow corridor.
Soon he was standing before a door. The sound of his heart
beating proved to Dao-sheng that this was real. Indeed, he
was more awake than he had ever been, as if brought into the
world for what was about to happen. The mountains he had
climbed and the rivers he had forded had led him here. Once
he had lived this moment, he could die without regret.

Lao Sun knocked at the door and drew back.

Xiao-fang appeared. "Come in, please."

It was the middle of winter, and the room was in shadow; the square window shades, partially scrolled down, were white by contrast. Echoing them in whiteness were the bed curtains at the far end of the room. They were closed; at first one would never have guessed anyone was behind them. As he neared, however, Dao-sheng could hear faint groans. Next to the bed, though positioned at a discreet distance, was a chair. Xiao-fang motioned Dao-sheng toward it. He sat down. The room's sober but harmonious atmosphere calmed him. He began to say in a resolute tone what he had rehearsed.

"Lady, I am a traveling doctor. My name is Dao-sheng. I have had extensive experience treating illness, and now I have the honor of examining you, to determine whether I might help. If I may be so bold, could you tell me a little about what you are suffering?"

The first sounds were muffled, but as she described her condition, the sick woman's diction grew clearer. This was not the first time that Dao-sheng had heard the voice, but it was the first time it was directed at him. It was weak but, to his ears, as pure as a trickle of rainwater.

"My illness has lasted for more than two months, and I have pain in several places. I often feel shortness of breath, heart palpitations, headaches combined with dizziness, and sharp stabs of pain on the side of the liver. My fever will not go down. I have tried medications and needles. They made me worse. I am afraid that I am a lost cause, Doctor."

"Allow me to determine that, my lady. Permit me to take your pulse."

From an opening in the bed curtain emerged a hand, coming to rest on the side of the bed. It was thin and pitifully pale, but

François Cheng

to Dao-sheng it seemed like an offering, the living embodiment of the most precious of all earthly treasures. He extended two fingers, his index and middle fingers, and pressed them tenderly to Lan-ying's wrist.

He thrilled at the sensation of touching, yet knew he could not enjoy it for its own sake; there were limits that were not to be surpassed. He collected his thoughts and focused them on the sounds and echoes coming through the arteries. Listening to the signals emitted by the five *zang,* or organs, and the six *fu,* or intestines, he learned which were functioning and which were obstructed. He listened to the song of the breaths, which wheezed and groaned as they flowed continuously across the meridians, finding their way into the body's smallest and most remote corners, from the top of the spinal column to the extremities of each limb. It bespoke inflamed tissue crying out to be refreshed. Corrupted blood waiting to be purified. This body that had known so many specific sicknesses was suffering from the accumulation of a lifetime of wounds and bitterness: the dream of communion with beauty that was dashed as soon as it had been expressed; the union in her marriage of ugliness and vulgarity; the agony of miscarriages; the experience of violence, abduction, and abandonment. Here was a life that had gone too long without happiness, perhaps even the hope of happiness in another life, whose reality she did not doubt.

Dao-sheng asked for the other hand. He heard the sound of a body turning, then a hand emerged from behind the curtain, coming to rest—just as the first had—on the side of the bed. Were it not so charged by suffering the motion would have had something graceful about it, something both as precise and as expressive as that of a musician or an actress in an opera. As before, Dao-sheng slowly moved his index and middle fingers and pressed them to the wrist, his thumb delicately supporting the back of the hand. Touching had almost become familiar, the kind of pleasure one feels when one runs into an old friend whom one had been hoping to see. Lan-ying seemed to demonstrate less timidity and reserve than before. Perhaps, thought Dao-sheng, she also was feeling as if she had come across an old friend and was allowing herself to enjoy the moment.

The left hand reinforced what he had learned from the right, as he noted the murmur echoing deep in the heart. He knew that he was taking more time than other doctors would in this examination of the pulse but did not sense that this was creating fear or doubt in his patient.

"As you yourself have said, my lady, your illness has a number of sources. It cannot be traced to any single one. This will require careful treatment, administered step by step. It would be best to deal with your general state immediately. After that, we can begin to cure the individual afflictions. Because normal medications and the needles have not had any effect, they should be discontinued. I will ask you to trust me, and to try several of my own mixtures. The treatment will take time. I can also tell you that there is hope. When I return to my monastery, I will prepare a potion. Then I will deliver it myself. It needs to be heated and taken morning and night. I will come back to see you in five days."

Dao-sheng indeed returned five days later. As before, after listening to Lan-ying speak of her condition, he took her pulse.

This taught him the exact state of her illness. Moreover, the long silent contact was in and of itself a kind of therapy, even to the point of—if only very minimally—transferring vital energy from one body to another. When the session was over, he explained to Lan-ying and Xiao-fang that, as there were faint signs of improvement, the potion should be administered for another five days.

During his next visit, Dao-sheng performed the same actions as before. Then he proposed that they now change the general medication for one that concentrated on the liver and kidneys. Before he took his leave, Lan-ying, from behind the curtain, asked Xiao-fang to offer Dao-sheng some tea. He accepted and took a seat at the table next to the window. While he was stirring his tea, Lan-ying hazarded a question. "Master, you are not from here. Where are you from?"

"I originally came from the Shu country but was taken away when a child. Since then I have been nearly everywhere."

"Why did you come to our town?"

"I came here in my youth. I was much taken with it."

A visit every five days would set the rhythm of an entire month. Each visit was as before, yet for Dao-sheng, who lived in a state of increasingly happy excitement, it was momentous. Beyond the fact that her health improved slowly but steadily, he noted that a certain understanding almost instinctively was beginning to grow between himself and Lan-ying. The few words they exchanged remained innocuous. Lan-ying learned a little about Dao-sheng's soothsaying practice or about what was happening at the temple. Following the strict rules governing such matters, he was not permitted to see his patient. She felt too weakened and pale to have wanted him to. Yet it was impossible for her to hide, or for him to fail to know, that she was allowing herself to be cared for.

Soon the year came to an end. The New Year celebrations left doctor and patient indifferent, so absorbed were they with fighting the illness whose roots went deeper than they had imagined, and which sometimes threatened to drag Lan-ying back down. The inexplicable relapses were always deeply worrisome. One day, when he was taking Lan-ying's pulse and feeling a certain anxiety, Dao-sheng decided to take advantage of Xiao-fang's momentary absence to say something. He had rehearsed the words in his mind and thus spoke in a calm, unhurried voice.

"More than thirty years ago, at the estate of the Lu family, the very venerable Old Lord was celebrating his seventieth birthday. After the banquet, a play was performed in the great room. A young girl in a red dress was listening from behind the screen. Do you remember?"

"It was one of the most beautiful moments of my life. Yet so brief. It vanished like a cloud. How do you know of this?"

"In the orchestra was a young violinist, sitting at the end of the row. You could see him from behind the screen. Do you remember?"

There came a slight tremor of the hand, denoting both surprise and the awareness that a revelation was imminent.

"I was young and innocent then," Lan-ying replied after a pause. "I knew nothing of life. I did see the young musician, and I have never forgotten him."

"Your name was Miss Lan-ying. The young musician would later be called Dao-sheng."

She opened the palm of her hand and let him press his to it. It was a silent moment of communion, of wordless ecstasy. The intimacy born of these two hands was as when two faces approach, or two hearts are imprinted upon each other. When the corolla of five petals unfolds, like a glove being turned inside out, it delivers up its secret depths, letting itself be nourished by the warm breeze, or bounced by eager butterflies and honeybees that light upon it. Between two hands with fingers interlaced a fluttering of wings produced a tiny shudder, the slightest pressure a wave that expanded in radiating circles. What one hand caressed was not simply another hand but the very caress of the other. They floated in a state that might have been dreamed of in infancy, or in a previous life. Intermingling veins, irrigating desire, attach themselves to life's deepest sources; the intersecting lines that foretell the future extend into the distance until they join with the infinity of the stars.

Hidden by the curtain, Lan-ying did not see their hands; Dao-sheng, however, did. He saw his own once delicate hand, callused over by years of labor, lying atop Lan-ying's slender white hand, from which, because of her illness, the bones protruded. There was undeniable contrast and yet, also, a harmony, due to the fact that each was absorbed in consoling the other. Lan-ying smoothed his rough skin. Dao-sheng believed that this hand, offered so tenderly, could be made healthy and full again. The soothsayer's voice whispered into the doctor's ear, "Now those predestined for each other truly have found each other. No obstacle and no illness can come between them."

Indeed, during the months to come, the medications and the power of love itself pulled Lan-ying back from the edge of the abyss. At each meeting, from behind the curtain, her hand willingly sought his. It was all that they could do. They knew how wildly audacious this was and at the same time how entirely and uniquely innocent. They nearly believed that what was occurring between them had never before happened, forgetting whether they were in the half-light of this room or someplace else, whether it was afternoon or morning. Destiny had reunited them, and enfolded them. Either they would obey it or they would create a whole new one. From within the crevices of the fluvial bed where it had dried out so many years before, words can issue forth again.

The circumstances in which they found themselves were unique, but both knew intuitively that now—or never—was the time to speak. At first, they shyly recalled their first meeting. Each word brought to the surface the flame of a memory, which, fed by other flames, lit up in all its original brightness the scene they had lived as if in a dream, yet a dream that had dominated their respective lives. Was it, they wondered, enough to remember those moments truly to find each other again? Each had lived a life in the years that had come after. And each life, with its crossings and detours, shed its own light.

Dao-sheng spoke first, for he already knew the broad outlines of Lan-ying's life, whereas she knew nothing at all of his. Slowly and yet without hesitation he launched into a fairly long retelling. The scenes connected and built up: the terror of being a child suddenly taken from his parents and thrown into the hard world of adults when he was sold to the theater troupe; the brutalizing rites of initiation; the luck of being spotted by one of the older men, who taught him to read and to play the violin; the evening when Second Young Lord Zhao had provoked him, and after the fight had had him condemned to forced labor in the regions of the North; the dangerous escape, followed by a period no less dangerous in which he went from town to town and, having to take whatever work he could find, was dragged down into the company of criminals; the decision to pull himself away from this dissolute life and climb Mount Huang; the new chance offered him, that of being accepted by the Taoist Great Master who taught him medicine and divination; the impossibility of his becoming a Taoist monk because of one memory he had never been able to let go of; the life of an itinerant doctor and soothsayer, an irrepressible longing to return locked in his heart.

"I am without ties or home. No parents and no relatives await me. My return was to a smile that once and forever blinded me to all else. That was where my life truly began, and that is where my life must end. Instinctively, I drew ever closer to the South. When I reached the shore of the Yangtze and saw the current, my heart leapt. All I had to do was cross the river to return to the place where the object of all my thoughts lived. Yet the first time I came to the southern bank, I lost faith. So I climbed up to the monastery on Mount Gan, and there I stayed for three years. Long enough for me to realize once and for all that the purpose of my life was to find you, even if I had no reason to hope."

Compared with this, Lan-ying's story seemed straightforward. But that was only an appearance. Her life, which should have been so easy, was fraught with frustrations and inner turmoil. She had also been marked by losses and threats. Her marriage had been a slow process of annihilation, of debasement and suspicion. Then came the miscarriages, the abduction. Spurred on by Dao-sheng's self-assurance and as if driven by some irresistible desire, she started to relate in fragments what had happened during her kidnapping. The long journey toward the mountain beneath an unforgiving sun; the torture of thirst; the porters who, when they were changing teams, threw the chair in which she was being carried in the air, for their own amusement as well as to terrify her. It took all her strength not to scream, so as not to incite them further. Then came the nights in the hut, guarded by two women whose loud snores mixed with the cries of the night birds, making her fear and anxiety almost unbearable.

"I thought about ways of ending my life should something terrible happen. I reviewed my miserable life, forgetting the only moments of happiness when I was a young girl, moments that seemed to have fallen from Heaven. What I most feared almost happened. Not all the bandits were evil. They were poor people pushed to their limits. But one of the chiefs was an animal, and one night he came into the hut shouting and reeking of alcohol. By luck, another chief came and stopped him, reminding him that if they wanted their ransom I was not to be touched. He knew my name, for a member of his family had once received charity from me. The Buddha's ray shone during even the darkest night."

When she had finished her story, told with a spontaneity and boldness that had taken her by surprise, Lan-ying was exhausted. She retreated into silence. All she could do was agree with a movement of her hand and a single word when Dao-sheng said, "We must thank Heaven and Earth that we have been united at last."

"Yes."

"What we have been through means nothing. We feel no regret because we are together again."

"Yes."

"We are together again. Never to part!"

"Yes."

Throughout this exchange Dao-sheng let himself be taken by the secret charm of his surroundings. He was in a woman's room, something he had thought would never be permitted him. The dresses in the colors of the four seasons hanging from the back of the screen; the unfinished embroidery sitting upon a small round table; the faint plume of smoke rising from the incense burner, thinner than the track of a tear; the spotless bed curtains with their faint orchid designs; and that plum tree outside, sketching a graceful silhouette on the window, like some remnant of an unrealized dream—as best he could, he stored all this in his memory, sensing that the circumstances in which he found himself had not been brought about by human means. And in all probability they would never again occur.

Lady Fu-chun usually stopped by in the morning to inquire after Lan-ying's health. She arrived unexpectedly one afternoon. Luckily, Dao-sheng was seated at the table writing down a list of medications to purchase. Responding to her implication that he was taking his time, he replied gravely that Lady Ying had come a long way—she had almost died, but thanks to Heaven she was at last on the road to recovery. Fu-chun mumbled her thanks and took her leave. Because of what he had just said, Dao-sheng knew that the time when he would no longer be able to come was fast approaching.

Eight

ONCE RECOVERED FROM HER ILLNESS, LAN-YING REMAINED IN her room for another dozen days. Finally, one morning, unable to resist the appeal of spring sunshine, she decided to go to the temple. After her many months of absence, the desire to show gratitude to Buddha was great. She had another reason to feel impatience, though she willed herself not to think about it, for she was intimidated by the idea of seeing again the man who from now on would occupy the very center of her life.

There were crowds as soon as one entered the town, and they were most dense in the region of the temple. The porters, Lao Sun and Zhu the Sixth, were used to it. They swerved to the right and to the left before succeeding in setting the chair down in front of the teahouse on the square facing the temple. Lan-ying and Xiao-fang emerged from the chair and made their way to the temple on foot. They needed only to turn their heads slightly to the right to locate Dao-sheng's stand. He was in the middle of a consultation with a client. Before coming, Lan-ying had tried to reconstitute the image of the man from her distant memories. Now there he was in the flesh. All she could really see from this angle was his profile. A long head, beard, hair pulled back and held in place by a wooden peg. Despite the decades of "wind and sand," the nobility of the face had not been eroded.

Inside the temple, the two women moved through the throng of worshippers toward the distant altar, on which sat a shining gold Buddha. They lit incense sticks and planted them on the tray filled with cinders, then got down on their knees and began their prayers. When they had finished, they returned to the center of the temple, where there were long benches. These were almost entirely filled, for it was the hour of the prenoon prayer. After much searching, the women found two free places. Before they had time to sit, however, a large procession of monks and bonzes arrived dressed in saffron; leading them was the Great Monk. They took their place on the riser stretching from one end of the altar to the other. While waiting for silence, the Great Monk gazed at the assembly. He saw Lan-ying and nodded and smiled his joy at seeing her well again. She responded with a gentle inclination of the head. When the ceremony began, she became happily immersed in the enveloping atmosphere of collective prayer: the darkness broken by iridescent flashes, the scent of candles and incense, the mesmerizing, psalmodic litanies punctuated by the crystalline tones of bells, and the deep tones made by the fish-shaped wooden *mu-yu* that kept time. When the ceremony was over, Lan-ying felt slightly weak. Good sense dictated waiting until the crowds had diminished before trying to make her way to the exit. Outside, the noonday bustle was at its height. As she descended the stairs she could see that now Dao-sheng was unoccupied, though around him strolled

François Cheng

curious passersby. Followed by Xiao-fang, she made her way resolutely toward a surprised Dao-sheng, smiled naturally, and said, "I have left my room for the first time. I came to thank you for having cured me."

As she spoke she looked closely at him, with his high forehead, his light eyebrows, and the expression of intelligence and sensitivity that animated his face. She was able to discern, for a brief instant, what had fascinated her so many years ago about the young musician who, leaning forward, had hummed to himself the melody he was playing.

"There is no need to thank me," Dao-sheng replied in a clear voice. "If the lady has recovered, it is the will of Heaven."

Then he, too, smiled. Their rather stiff formulations were intended for people listening; their message for each other was in their smiles, which would be their sole form of communication.

The news that Lady Ying had been to the temple traveled quickly. The poor knew that soon they could return to the back gate of the Zhao estate for food, and indeed at long last the Great Monk, having been so informed by Lao Sun, announced that such was the case. Those who used to gather there assembled once again.

At first, Dao-sheng hesitated about rejoining them. It was when he noted that some of these destitute people were sick, aged, and infirm that he overcame his scruples. It was in the Buddhist tradition of charity to help those who needed it. And it was in that tradition that he appeared openly before Lan-ying. He said "thank you" as he lifted his bowl in the gesture of a supplicant, and Lan-ying invariably replied, "Don't thank me. Thank Buddha." They pronounced these words with dignity and gratitude, genuinely persuaded that their ability to exchange a look and a smile every day was thanks to divine beneficence.

One day, after the food distribution at the end of the second month and during weather of particular mildness, Lan-ying and Xiao-fang as usual crossed the garden to return to their chambers. They stopped on the path, suddenly taken by the sight of the growing *chun-ya*, spring flowers, and *di-cai*, small green vegetables.

"Oh, what a long time it has been since I've seen these rare creatures!" exclaimed Lan-ying. "They grow only in spring, and they're good enough for imperial palate."

She bent down to pick them. The two women came back to the kitchen with their hands full. Lan-ying was inspired. "Starting tomorrow we must improve and vary the vegetables. We must not forget to add what the seasons provide—mushrooms, bamboo shoots, golden needles, lotus roots . . ."

The following day, during the food distribution, someone who was getting his bowl filled exclaimed, "This smells really good! It's like a feast day!"

Xiao-fang smiled, as did Lan-ying.

The next in line echoed the refrain. "Absolutely no doubt about it! Lady Ying is cheerful for the first time!"

With that came general laughter, spreading the feeling that on this fallow little corner of the world truly there was a feast.

On her way back to her rooms, Lan-ying was in a light-hearted mood. The flowering plants and bushes all along the green path were dancing with butterflies. One of the largest and most glorious of them had landed on a dahlia. Xiao-fang crept up to catch it, but it flew away.

Lan-ying consoled her. "Why catch it? Let living things live as they will."

When they returned to the house, Lan-ying went directly to her armoire and took out a box of jewels. After rummaging through them, she extracted a silver brooch. It was in the shape of a butterfly.

Xiao-fang was so delighted she jumped up and clapped her hands. "How beautiful it is! I've never seen you wear it!"

"It was a gift from my mother when I was married. I wore it for a while, then put it away and forgot all about it."

"Put it on so that I can see it."

"Put it on? At my age?"

"The butterfly has no age. It's new each year. You're getting younger and younger, too. I can see it. I say, like a butterfly you must follow your heart. What is good and beautiful has no age."

Lan-ying returned to the temple several days later. When she was leaving she passed by Dao-sheng's stand; he was just then speaking with a client. Out of discretion she gave a simple nod. Lifting his head, Dao-sheng saw her radiant face and, in her hair, a butterfly. He smiled, inclining his head to show his appreciation. Alerted by this gesture, his client turned around. Struck by Lan-ying's beauty, he followed her with his eyes until she disappeared into the crowd.

Without changing his expression, and with a tone of serious-ness, Dao-sheng explained. "That is a lady of the Zhao house-hold who has just recovered from a grave illness, thanks to

Heaven. Do you not agree that a woman's beauty truly comes from Heaven? When she recovers it, it becomes more precious than all the gold in the world."

The client agreed with vigorous nodding of the head. It was the scholar, a cultivated man. He was a *xiu-cai,* a bachelor of letters, a perpetual taker of the examinations for higher degrees.

Dao-sheng commented on this. "Will this not be the ninth time that you have taken the mandarinal examination?"

"It will."

"And if you fail yet again, will you feel as if your life has been a failure?"

"I will. Wise men have said that any man worthy of his name must serve. He must participate third, behind the work of Heaven and of Earth. My way of offering service will be by attaining a position and through my writings."

"Your ambition honors you. But is it not possible to change your way of looking at things? For example, not to use the mandarinal examination as a measure. These examinations are not the result of heavenly decree; they are made by men. They are governed by outdated rules, not to mention affected by the inevitable abuses. I hope I do not offend you by saying that those poems you have written that follow the prescribed rules are not as good as those you have written spontaneously, which have touched me deeply. They reveal something unique to you. Truly a gift from Heaven. You must trust me: That gift is as precious as beauty is to a woman."

"I am grateful for these words of comfort. But how can you be sure of this gift? How can you find it?"

"I believe that rather than seeking it from without, in the

reactions of others, you have to look deep within yourself, down to the very source from which what is unique springs. Just as a woman's beauty always comes from within, not from makeup."

"You may be right. But I am afraid that without official recognition, the gift cannot reveal its worth."

"Mandarinal recognition is not the only kind. Life offers all sorts of possibilities, and there are other ways of finding expression for these gifts. Once I was a promising musician and had achieved some acclaim. People enjoyed my playing. But destiny had other plans. After a misfortune, I led a hard life that ruined my hand and I could no longer be a musician. Someone else might have been consumed by despair. But by perseverance I eventually found those careers that have brought you to me—medicine and divination. I bring to them the best I have to offer: a bit of intelligence, a bit of sensibility, much concentration and devotion. However, you don't even need to change professions. Your talent is literary. If you pass the examinations this time, fine. If not, your best writings will still give joy to your contemporaries and dazzle generations to come. It will be—as you put it—your way of offering service."

The scholar had no words with which to respond. He paid for the consultation and with slow steps moved off.

The days passed. The glory of spring ebbed, saving its most dazzling explosions of color for last. Dao-sheng and Lan-ying felt joy at the limited happiness now accorded them: the daily meetings behind the Zhao estate and those—less frequent— near the temple steps. They could hazard only tiny exchanges, but the smallest word, the briefest look, the least gesture were all accorded full significance, lifting the couple toward a sphere whose reality they sensed confusedly. Dao-sheng no longer counted the days; his life was anchored upon the regular apparition of her presence, unchanging and yet always renewing. Her body sometimes stirred his. When he dared acknowledge it, what he felt was desire, desire to caress again the hand of the woman—or the woman herself—so smooth and so sweet, so willing, and at moments so ingeniously alive. He felt that he had entered into more harmonious resonance with her.

He had been with women before, without truly appreciating what it meant. There was a lost period following his escape when he frequented the neighborhoods of ill repute in the towns of the North. Now, for the first time, he was reflecting upon what is feminine. He had the revelation that a woman's charm, when not debased by outside things, comes from her being able to transform virtually everything into music. She is made of flesh, of course, but this flesh gets transmuted into murmurs, perfumes, and radiances in waves that are endless but do not muffle the music. A woman's body is nature's miracle. Or, more precisely, it is the nature within the body that is miraculous, for there can be found all of nature's wonders: Gentle rolling hills, hidden valleys, springs and expanses, flowers and fruit. One should treat this body as if it were a landscape. As the Taoist master has taught, in a landscape one learns to commune not with the elements but with what emanates from them—the green light of the monsoons, the breezes moaning in the pine trees, the odors of sap carried by fog and wind.

Dao-sheng was saving up for the time when there would be nothing, and he learned to savor these things with patient slowness. Not able to touch her, he felt the curious sensation that he was pushing deeper into what was really the essence of woman, understanding her emanations. He fell into the rhythmic waves of Lan-ying's presence, produced by the breath and the fluids circulating within her, and these led with surprising certainty to secret ecstasy.

Such ecstasy could also be brought about by simple recognition. Like the day when Lan-ying and Xiao-fang went to the temple accompanied by Gan-er. When the boy saw Dao-sheng, he exclaimed, "Why, it's the man who came to the house to take care of Lady Ying! Here he is, right in the middle of the street! What a great spot. You can sit here and watch everything all day long. I want to become a soothsayer like him!"

This elicited a long loud laugh from Xiao-fang, and a more discreet one from her mistress. "You'd better figure out what you want to do in life," the maid said to the young man, wiping her tears of laughter. "Only a little while ago in the temple you thought the monks' chant so beautiful that you were convinced you'd become a bonze!"

Nine

THE GARDEN ONE CROSSED TO REACH THE ZHAOS' BACK GATE
would have reverted to a state of wilderness had Lao Sun not
decided to tend to it occasionally, when and as the mood struck
him. Formerly, Lan-ying crossed through with a hurried step,
always sticking to the path, looking neither left nor right. She
avoided those parts that might signal the change of seasons—
for fear of giving rise within her to feelings of melancholy or
nostalgia. Now, however, she slowed her progress, and had to
will herself to return to her rooms after the food distribution.

The summer had reached its height. The vegetal world was
displaying the full range of its treasures of sight and smell. The
whole length of the garden path was clotted with weeds inter-
mixed with tiny flowers. Lan-ying stopped and began pulling out
the taller ones with her hands. She discovered they were hardier
than she had thought. Witness to her mistress's painful attempts
at weeding, Xiao-fang ran toward a shed located not far from the
back gate and returned with a number of implements—scythes
and shears. Without asking for assistance, the two women

applied themselves diligently to clearing the whole path. After two or three days of hard work, it looked as it had in former times.

Encouraged by the result—though it had been accomplished at the cost of many scratches and small cuts—Lan-ying, with Xiao-fang's help, also tended the groups of wildflowers and shrubs. She tore off dead branches, snipped or repaired broken twigs, and watered the flowers that required the most care, such as the peonies, dahlias, and chrysanthemums. She grew to recognize every flower's face and to know each of their names. When she called to them, she thought she could hear them answer, addressing her as Lan-ying—"slender orchid." She had been called that as a child. After her marriage, she had taken the more respectable name Ying-niang, or Lady Ying. Being called Lan-ying now by someone who knew her only by this name and, for his whole life, had held to it, gave it even greater impact. This name so charged with the thought of the other filled her entirely—like this garden, whose flowers were recovering both their beauty and their name. She had aged, undeniably. Yet those lost years were like a nightmare; once woken from, it could no longer thwart the reawakening of youth.

She would undertake to bring the garden back to life—her half of it, of course. The other half was Second Lord's domain. Looking out the window from his room, he could take in that part of the garden. Lan-ying rarely ventured there. The two halves were divided by a row of trees—pagodas, acacias, pines, and poplars—that bordered the path on the right, and that in high summer formed a natural screen, dispensing generous shade and freshness. From one of the acacia branches hung a swing whose ropes had been blackened by weather. Now used only by children, it might tempt older people as well were it made new again.

For the moment, Lan-ying had plenty to do on the left side of the path. Her fiefdom was very full. Indeed, she thought it the finest part of the entire garden. In addition to the abundant plants and flowers, there was the artificial mountain, made up of stacked boulders, and further off, a pond, which for the moment was in a pitiful state. A few sallow-looking lotus flowers languished on the stagnant water. She asked Lao Sun and Zhu the Sixth to restore the pond. They drained it and unblocked the channel. They replaced old stones and planted new lotus flowers. Soon goldfish and dragonflies animated the clear water with their movements. Borne by the larger leaves, down which droplets of water rolled like pearls, the lotus flowers, having reached maturity, unfolded to the full extent of their magnificence. The whitest among them rivaled in airy grace the puffy clouds reflected in the water; with their light pink outer petals and their carmine cores, the red ones were as compelling as flesh.

The days of summer lengthened and slowed; the afternoons seemed never-ending. Lan-ying's life turned monotonous. Days inside were spent sewing or doing embroidery, making mufflers and shoes. She joined in the preparation of dinner, which took up some time. The food distribution and the visits to the temple were her only excursions into the outside world, and they were always over too soon. She could resist no longer the call of the outdoors. When Xiao-fang was off doing the laundry or shopping in town, Lan-ying adopted the habit of leaving her room and, as if obeying some command she could not resist, heading straight for the pond. There she felt in unison with the songs of the birds and the buzzing of the bees. In the blinding heat of the day, she became intoxicated with the smell of grass pushing up through the cracked soil. Seated on the bank, she distractedly struck at the surface with a willow branch, producing circles of water. Traversed by goldfish, they expanded eccentrically. She felt peace here. And yet—doubts and fears, thoughts struggling to be formulated, troubled the serenity of even these moments.

How marvelous this little corner of garden is, sheltered from everything, Lan-ying reflected. The lotus shadow is so attractive, the chatter of the orioles so pleasant. All these things seem to rejoice with happiness at being here. That is all that needs saying. What is it that men look for on earth? They do not feel the same languid happiness about life as plants do. The truth is the opposite—only a tiny few are content. Buddha teaches us that unhappiness reigns here. Yet more unhappy is the fate of women. Well, if everything is unhappiness, nothing more needs saying. That among this unhappiness a miracle would arise, and that it would happen in my life—it is so difficult to understand! My youthful innocence was so dreamlike. I thought it gone forever, like smoke, and yet thirty years later it returns. The man of my dreams entered my room and sat close to me. Even now he is not far—just beyond the wall. Thirty years ago we saw each other for the space of one evening, but we could not forget. How could we do so now, when we see each other nearly every day? This is happiness. What misery that our time together is so brief, and that we can exchange only courtesies. In unhappiness we discover happiness, and in happiness we suffer. It is so difficult to understand. Will life go on like this? How it would help me to speak with Dao-sheng. He is a soothsayer and must see matters more clearly. . . .

At this point in her thoughts, Lan-ying shuddered. A thought stirred within her: Who has made me so bold as to act so outrageously? I was a girl from a good family. I am a married woman. How is it possible that I let myself behave in this manner?

Lan-ying's thoughts grew shrouded in worry. During the days that followed, they returned to this line of reflection; nighttime was worse. She was knotted up inside and had no one to turn to. The only person close to her was Xiao-fang. Though she had complete confidence in her maid, Lan-ying doubted whether she should share her worries with her. It would be more than a matter of opening her mouth—broaching a subject that was so deeply shocking.

In the end Xiao-fang herself forced her mistress to open her heart. She had of course noted Lady Ying's pensive air, as well as her sudden reluctance to go to the temple. Xiao-fang had her feet on the ground and exhibited unswerving good judgment in practical matters. Though she also never lacked in delicacy and discretion, when it came to matters of the heart, she got straight to the point. Being independent-minded was probably behind her determination to remain single. She saw what happened to women when they married. Since she had started to work for the Zhao family, she had devoted herself body and soul to Lady Ying, ignoring her mistress's advice during the early years not to exclude the possibility of starting her own family. She helped her lady with daily chores, accompanied her when she went out, cared for her when she was sick, bathed her, and helped her to bed. In Lady Ying's moments of darkness, Xiao-fang was a steady stream of light to her.

Xiao-fang made Lady Ying's marital troubles her own, and she would do the same with this exceptional adventure involving Dao-sheng. Without understanding the finer points of love, yet full of sympathy and understanding, Xiao-fang had her own ideas on the subject, ideas inspired by her fervent wish to ease her mistress's anxiety.

Taking advantage of an appropriate moment, she jumped straight in. "Your behavior shocks you because you think you belong to a respectable family. We all know what dreadful things Second Lord has done. There are, I'm sure, many we don't know about. Look at what he did to Dao-sheng, for example. Had Dao-sheng not told us what happened to him years ago, we never would have known. The Heavens seemed to watch over him, for they let him come back. When you were rescued from the bandits, the Great Monk offered a proverb: 'He that survives a great calamity will later find great happiness.' I believe that's what is happening to you. Why shouldn't we say what's true? Second Lord gave you up. He stopped caring about you. How can we forget how long it was before he paid the ransom? I know he was in a pitiful state. But your life was at stake! And when you became so sick, he didn't seem much worried. He sent Lady Fu-chun to check on you. Her voice always sounded false when she asked how you were. I will say one thing more. The other day I thought to myself,

François Cheng

Well, after all, Dao-sheng and you, you met before you were married. It's as if you were destined for each other. If only the Heavens had arranged things differently!"

Lan-ying smiled, and though it was a rueful smile it denoted that Xiao-fang's honesty had touched her. She sighed. "Yes, before my marriage. How one would like to believe in a *yuan*, in something preordained. It all seems far away, as if in a former life. So many things have happened. I can see that Dao-sheng has changed, yet without having changed completely. He fell into darkness and still he remained the man he was, as pure and true as before and—"

Xiao-fang couldn't stop herself from interrupting. "Lady Ying also changed, yet without having changed completely. You have remained as pure and as true as you were before!"

This woman who had changed without changing had not escaped the notice of the one sitting by the open window. Second Lord had locked his eyes upon this apparition of freshness that appeared and then disappeared down below the curtain of trees, this irresistible vision of charm in a light green dress. She was there again, stopping before one of the long-stemmed peonies, lingering long enough for him to see her face. The effects of age did not seem—inasmuch as these things could be observed from a distance—to have diminished the inner elegance of years before. In no way eclipsed by the magnificence of the flowers, she irradiated that mysteriously transparent and serene power of flesh secretly in bloom.

"What amazing creatures women are!" said Second Lord to

himself. "It is said 'a woman changes eighteen times.' Yet here is no young girl. When a woman nearing fifty is transformed in this way, it surpasses understanding. Becoming ugly is normal. Growing more beautiful? This I cannot understand. What has happened to her?"

Ten

THE ADVENT OF THIS COMPLETELY UNEXPECTED PHENOMENON dissipated the listlessness in which Second Lord had been stewing day after day, month after month. Now his existence could be summed up in the statement "Having seen once creates the desire to see again." Each day at the approach of noon he demanded to be carried to the window. Thus positioned, trying to hide his excitement by assuming a distracted air, he began his observation session.

Lady Fu-chun was delighted with her husband's new habit, for it granted her a break from having to devote every moment of her life to him. "How nice to sit near the window," she said. "The air is better! Staying in bed too long eventually causes fatigue."

Second Lord mumbled a few remarks about the nice weather and the flowers, but his attention was focused outside. Was that a light shadow moving among the trees? No, it was not yet midday; he would have to wait a bit longer. He waved a hand toward the center of the room, signifying that he wished to be left alone.

Patience was required—patience that demanded constant vigilance. From the moment he caught sight of her, first the profile, then her back as she walked with rapid steps toward the back gate, he would have to remain fully alert so as not to miss her return. With luck, the return trip would be, as it often was, unhurried; the lady appeared to take pleasure in the garden at this time of year. Seeing her face was not as easy as one might imagine. Second Lord had to sit up as straight as he could in his chair and crane his neck so that he could peer over the window ledge, all the while being very cautious not to be seen. The object of his lust, this creature flowering so fully and temptingly before his eyes, could conceal itself behind branches and foliage; it was like playing hide-and-seek with an invisible partner. At a certain moment, however, her form came fully into his view, appearing between sunlit tree trunks. So hard did Second Lord concentrate his gaze that it hurt his eyes. He knew the vision would not last long. And when, too soon, it disappeared, leaving a bitter taste in his open, panting mouth, it had the same effect as when someone dying of hunger prepares to devour a succulent dish only to have it whisked away at the last minute.

The absence might last even longer if by ill chance the woman decided to return home behind the artificial mountain. Then the voyeur's nerves were put to a brutal test, for he couldn't relax his attention; everything depended upon not missing the moment when she reappeared. No effort was negligible; each and every one might produce unexpected delights. Such discipline merited a reward. Now back within view, the desired body bent over to look for something among the grasses—a wildflower, perhaps. He let his eyes rest upon

François Cheng

the shapely contours of her thighs. Women! Meaning to or not, they can assume positions that dizzy the head. Other surprises, just as divine: With Xiao-fang and Gan-er at her side, she might run with her arms up to catch a butterfly in flight; or holding on to the ropes with her white hands, swing on the swing, and the edge of her dress might flutter up. . . .

The man jiggled in his chair and talked to himself in the way he used to with his cronies. "I'll admit there was a time when she pleased me. I was young then. I soon realized that it isn't enough for a woman to be pretty. She also has to know how to flatter. To be playful and resourceful in bed. If she just lies there, cold and silent, stiff as a plank, even a goddess is useless. Then came one miscarriage, then another, and it all got worse. A mournful look and the air of revulsion, and a man can't perform. No wonder I started going a little crazy. She wouldn't reply yes or no, no matter how much I shouted at her. She just sat there. She became ugly. I started going after the servant girls and visiting the brothels. Yes, I took some concubines. So what? She didn't exist for me anymore. I didn't even want to see her. I let her have her own side of the estate and gave her Xiao-fang to wait on her. Leave me in peace. Then she got kidnapped, and those bastards wanted me to pay an outrageous amount to get her back. We hesitated a little. Not enough to make anyone think we were heartless. I was barely alive myself. And we paid up in the end—a little less than what they wanted, thanks to Great Monk, who guaranteed that she had not been touched. I'm sure he was right. Her look would discourage an entire regiment of horny soldiers. After she came back, I left her more alone than ever. As things are, I have to rely on Fu-chun's care. I must say she's very good at it. But I'm not stupid. I know very well when she's faking it. With someone as battered as I am, a woman isn't getting what she wants. . . ."

With their highs and their lows, Second Lord's days passed by. One afternoon, when he was once again sitting alert and motionless in his chair in front of the window, a single thought obsessed him. It was like a tiresome fly: The more it was chased off the quicker it came back.

What does all this mean? What exactly has taken place here? What has happened to Lady Ying and therefore to me? This woman whom I married with such ceremony before the eyes of the world has become a stranger. It would be natural if she was wrinkled and deformed. Instead she has become bewitching and yet also beyond my grasp, and this I cannot understand. I cannot accept it! What does she do all day? I know the basics, of course. She does the same thing, more or less. She gives food to the poor, she goes to the temple and lights incense. Nothing special about all that. The rest of the time she goes round and round the garden until I get dizzy.

I must do something. I'm stuck here. I feel like I'm living the parable of the farmer sitting under a tree, waiting for the hare, when my blood is boiling. This is not a life. It is worse than a bath!

That thought brought resolution. He felt the desire to go out, head into town, immerse himself in life if only for an instant. It was desire such as he hadn't felt since becoming paralyzed. He wondered whether he could appear in public, or maybe meet up with his old colleagues in debauchery. It had been a long time since one of them had come knocking at his door. When he had happened to run into one of them, before he was paralyzed, the most he would offer was a polite word or two. He knew that now they would make fun of him behind his back. He could already guess what kind of lewd comments they would exchange. "How do you think Second Lord does it with a woman? He can't move. Can he still get it up?"

The good old days! They went from red palace to green pavilion, the wine flowed, the card games lasted all night, and the girls were there whenever you wanted them. How heartbreaking that it was all behind him now.

Second Lord was the first to be surprised by his urge to venture out. Did he have the heart for it? There would be no question of his revealing himself to anyone. If he went out, he would remain in the chair. From behind the curtain he could gaze at his leisure at what was going on around him. What would take courage would be watching the world rushing from one place to the other, happily going about its business. That would be almost too much to bear. Without some powerful motivation, he would never voluntarily dare to face the outside world.

Now he had the motivation: To observe Lady Ying. To really see all of her—and not in some intermittent, fragmentary sort of way but fully, entirely, and in bright light. To see what she was doing, and how she held herself, and how she walked. To reach out and snatch a piece of this hidden mystery. To reach in and pull out something he could sink his teeth into.

At this point in his thoughts, Second Lord felt compelled to face the truth: Though he had abused many women during his life, he had never truly *seen* them. Women were attractive flesh he had wanted to devour. Would he really have the patience to look at a woman calmly, humbly, silently? To see how she lived, how she dreamed, how she collected and transformed herself? To hear the rhythms of her life and learn how she filled her space—like a fan, from whose folds radiated beauty?

All this required rising to another order of things, one beyond the realm of Second Lord.

From Lao Sun and Zhu the Sixth's absence, Second Lord knew that Lady Ying had gone to the temple. To use the other chair, he would have to ask the two porters for help. These men were not young. Still, he knew that they would perform this task without great effort, so weightless had their master become.

Lady Fu-chun came back from visiting the neighbors. The news of what was happening took her by complete surprise, though her look of amazement soon melted into a smile. "Of course!" she exclaimed. "What a good idea to get out and see the world a little!"

This outing Second Lord was proposing would offer her a real reprieve. For a short while, at least, she wouldn't have to listen to him complain, or bring him tea, or light his pipe, or massage his neck and various other parts.

For all that the two porters took every conceivable precaution, there was nothing they could do to prevent the chair from being jostled, jangling Second Lord's nerves. Finally, with a groan of relief, they set the chair down in the place their master designated. It was a little off to the side but still close enough to afford an ample view of the square and the temple. The porters crouched behind the chair and lit their pipes, commenting to each other about what was going on around them. Protected from view, Second Lord took in the sounds, colors, and especially the smells assailing him from all directions. The constant motion of passersby made them seem like fish in an aquarium. They aimed for specific points yet made wide arcs to avoid bumping into one another. Paralyzed for so long, he was astounded by their agility.

Looking further away, he saw that people were starting to emerge from the temple, a sign that the ceremony was nearly over. Indeed Lady Ying soon emerged, followed by Xiao-fang. Her appearance as well as the grace with which she descended the stairs stirred him. At last he could see all of her.

From the depths of her luminous simplicity came an almost unimaginable sovereignty. The Great Monk was talking to her. He had the gall to talk to a saint! Well, perhaps he was right to, after all. She brought to mind Guan-yin, goddess of the Buddhist pantheon, the subject of so many paintings and statues. The image of Guan-yin sent a painful tremor through Second Lord's body.

"What have I become?" he asked himself out loud. "Even apart from the matter of my paralysis, how can I attain this woman's level? How can I impose myself upon her? My teeth are yellowed from opium. The skin on my cheeks is leathery; they're like slices of dried meat. The few strands of hair I have left are as white as a tuft of grass in winter."

Lady Ying had reached the bottom of the steps. She turned to the right, where there was a stand, and gestured to someone sitting behind it. "Who?" Second Lord asked himself. "Ah yes. That soothsayer, the one who also practices medicine. One of those charlatans who sometimes actually manages to cure someone. Yes, well, he made her better, and we shouldn't expect anything more, I suppose. Now she's turning to the right. Going where? Ah. Back to the chair. Lao Sun and Zhu the Sixth must have just come out of the teahouse."

Eleven

THE ARRIVAL OF WINTER SLOWED THE PACE OF HUMAN activity. With the New Year began a new cycle. A somewhat late spring did not alter the calendar, which followed its inexorable course. *Qing-ming*, the Festival of Sacrifice to the Dead celebrated in the third month of the year, came and went, and with it the time when the rains held sway. Finally the weather began to clear and the days grew milder. It was the time of the *Duan-wu*, the Festival of the Dragon, on the fifth day of the fifth month, and then suddenly it was the start of summer. During the day the town was alive with activity, for this was a period of respite from fieldwork, and the local farmers went to sell things in the market and to sell or exchange cattle, or to have their hard-used tools fixed, or to stock up on oil, salt, and tea.

It remained a troubled time. All that was left of the Ming Dynasty was the name, which means "clarity." Corruption was rampant, from the royal court down to the lowest social ranks. Taxes and tariffs rose. There had been many years of crop failure in various parts of the country. Everywhere there were rumors of uprisings and rebellions. This region of the country, better off than others, had its share of bankruptcy and lawlessness. Because of this, the police had recruited reinforcements and garrisoned them in the district capital. The populace there and in the neighboring towns thus enjoyed peace—though no one knew how long it would last. The lives of the common people became more and more difficult. Yet, for all that, it did not seem as if they had lost any of their vitality. The streets were clogged with carriages and carts. As the weather turned hot, people became even more animated, wearing brightly colored clothing. Women put on dresses that shimmered with light. On every street corner were stands overflowing with fruit—the medlar fruit and cherries competed in freshness; quartered watermelons flaunted their bloodred flesh.

Lady Ying's visits to the temple grew more frequent. She also stayed longer, because the number of worshippers had increased during this period and the ceremonies as a result were more prolonged. Second Lord's sorties kept pace. Despite the discomforts caused by being forced to wait longer, he wouldn't relent, though some—perhaps even himself—might have wondered why. Little or nothing changed in his wife's routine. What there was to see was fed by his imagination, and his excitement reached its climax every time she appeared at the top of the temple steps. To say that she stood out among other women was to say little. As she descended the steps with her natural grace and her shining face, one sensed that she had an inner rhythm, of which she herself was probably unaware. How unfortunate that it did not last long. As soon as she reached the base of the steps, she became less discernible.

You could see her pass before the stand, gesturing to the one sitting behind it; sometimes, if the man was busy with someone, she made no sign at all, simply glancing his way.

"This so-called Taoist may practice medicine," Second Lord said to himself, "but he is first and foremost a soothsayer. Apparently she never thinks of asking him for a prediction. I'm the one who needs one. I would like to know how much time I have left to live. Yes, that's it. I will obtain a prediction. Not right away. No. Lady Ying must not know that I am following her."

Waiting longer for Lady Ying to finish her prayers may have created something of a hardship for Second Lord, but it was a singular boon to his wife's porters, Lao Sun and Zhu the Sixth—particularly to Lao Sun, to whom it gave the first opportunity he'd had all day to eat. Zhu the Sixth's gratitude was more measured. He had gotten into the habit of coming to town after dinner, looking for amusement. Nonetheless, how could he turn down an offer to drink a few glasses in the teahouse with his colleague while they waited for their mistress to emerge from the temple?

These two men, strikingly different in character, had until now barely gotten to know each other. Lao Sun, the older, was from the countryside. He had come to the Zhao house after going from village to village trying to flee famine. Slow of speech and movement, he was honest to the core and enjoyed the complete confidence of his masters. Zhu the Sixth had grown up in the city. He was smooth-tongued and articulate, and quick both in his retorts and in the execution of his duties.

Honesty was not his strong suit, however, though he managed to keep this hidden. He had been hired by First Lord because of his skill in the martial arts. In days past he had served in the police, the *ya-men,* but had not thrived under the strict discipline. His current work, though sometimes irksome, suited him better because it left him free in the evenings to pursue his own pleasures.

On this particular day, bright sunlight flooded the square in front of the teahouse. The atmosphere inside was no less cheerful. The owner and her two daughters, wearing light blouses and with bare arms, moved between the tables in the noisy smoke-filled room. When they collected bowls and plates, the sound of clacking ivory porcelain seemed to emphasize the tenderness of their skin.

"Ah, women," murmured Zhu the Sixth, feeling agreeably tipsy.

"What about women?"

"Besides them, what is there? I ask you. So what about you, Lao Sun? What has your life been like? I bet you're still a virgin. Holding out for someone special?"

"I'm from the country. Famine forced me from my village. I'm lucky to be alive. I've been at the Zhaos' for sixteen years. I'm almost forty."

"Never thought of taking a wife?"

"A poor man like me?"

"Being poor doesn't keep you from wanting a woman, does it?"

"Well, actually, there is someone."

"Aha! Who?"

"I don't know if I should tell you."

"Oh, come on. Who is it?"

"Well, actually, it's Shun-zi," replied Lao Sun. "You remember Shun-zi? She was the one abused by Second Lord and later sold to a brothel."

"I know her."

"When I arrived at the Zhaos' I didn't have a single coin to my name. I didn't dare think anything, or do anything, let alone talk of taking a wife. But I fell in love with her the moment I saw her, with her bangs and her beautiful eyes, her dimples. She was so adorable it broke my heart. Her voice was so sweet. When that terrible thing happened to her, I almost couldn't believe it. Lady Fu-chun went nuts. Then Second Lord sold her. Later she was sold again, to a brothel. I was a fool for not having tried to marry her."

"Too late now."

"Maybe not."

"What do you mean? She's a whore."

"You say 'whore.' I say she is a prostitute. You can buy back a prostitute, from what I'm told."

"Listen to you! You can't marry a whore! You're strange, Lao Sun."

"I'm in love with a woman, that's all."

"Have you gone to see her?"

"Not yet. Visiting a brothel is a . . . shameful thing."

"You want to buy back Shun-zi and you're too ashamed to go and see her! How do you expect to succeed? Listen, I've been to some brothels. I used to go all the time. Now . . . less often. You see, there are other ways of finding women, easier ways that are also cleaner and don't cost you anything."

"Easier ways of finding women?"

"Oh, yes indeed, my good friend Lao Sun. You're an honest man. Too honest to know how to get your hands on a woman. It's not that hard."

"What do you mean?"

"Take me. I'm young, but I've already had my share. I used to be in the *ya-men*. Now, like you, I work for the Zhao family. Tomorrow, I don't know where I'll be. Wherever I go I'll find a way. Even with a face like this, women are attracted to me."

"But to get your hands . . . like you say . . . How do you do that?"

"You have to know how to look, how to talk, and how to appear sure of yourself. All you need is to find an attractive woman, wait for the right moment, and say just the right thing to her. Sometimes you have to repeat it a few times. She won't get tired of it. Believe me. Watch."

Lao Sun turned and saw that one of the proprietor's daughters was heading their way with a fresh pitcher of wine. When she put it on the table and replaced the bowls before them, Zhu the Sixth said smoothly and in a low voice, "Pretty miss, your hands are so white and delicate—finer than any porcelain."

The girl blushed, glanced at him hastily, and left.

"See what I mean? Do that with a girl, and you'll end up having your way with her."

"Easy in a teahouse. It wouldn't work anywhere else."

"Lao Sun, you are, as I said, an honest fellow, but you're not nearly crafty enough. Listen to me. There are women everywhere. And there are all sorts of ways of getting to them. They're doing the wash at the river's edge, or bringing food to the workers in the fields, or strolling through the markets and maybe they need help carrying things, or looking for someone to help them across a bridge. You just have to know how to get close and say the right thing. If by chance she responds with a sign and you manage to see her again, you've got it made. Go slow. The worst thing you can do is push things too fast. It's all about persevering. A woman isn't like a dog or a horse. You can't just call and expect her to come running."

"I'm glad you've still got at least some respect for women."

"'Respect.' Not a word I would use. Let's put it this way: A woman is a woman."

"You have a mother."

"Never knew her. Died when I was two . . . I don't know why, but you know, I prefer older women. Widows. Married women."

"Married women? You've got nerve."

Zhu the Sixth was now fully soused, not just with wine but with himself, and his appreciation for his own seductive charm. He leaned near Lao Sun. "Yeah, I've got balls. You bet. Know what? I've done things with Lady Fu-chun!"

"*What?*"

"Don't tell anyone."

"Believe me, I won't. If I did, it would cost us our lives."

Twelve

THE AFTERNOON GREW HOT AND MOIST. THE DAYLIGHT HAD swollen to haziness, spreading its sensual languor. In the garden of the Zhao estate, the plants and trees, parched to stiffness, seemed to be holding their breath, as if in anticipation. Anticipation of what? The arrival of a storm, perhaps—one that might come from the gray clouds massing lazily in a corner of the sky. Suspended above, their demeanor was still uncertain. Nothing was certain at this moment. Desire floated vaguely in the air, and in the general torpor no one could formulate it with any clarity.

Nearer by, nonetheless, the sun's rays, without losing their blinding brightness, were filtered by something earthly, dusty. Wasps and flies hummed to exhaustion. A crow landed noisily on some branches, then took off again at full speed. The air made things worse. The only creature seemingly unaffected was a caterpillar, making its way across some moss at the foot of a mulberry tree. Crawling was its destiny. It would never have occurred to it to alter its movement. Even had the sky collapsed around it, the caterpillar would have given no sign of accelerating; its majestic dignity was stupefying.

Through the open window, at which sat Second Lord, the heavy perfume of flowers came in gusts. Perspiring lightly, he was overtaken by a strange sensation, one that had been stifled for a very long time. Ancient lecher turned apathetic, he felt within him something mounting, something of which he had thought himself no longer capable. He knew its root: a year's accumulation of desires, ceaselessly rising up and then being reined in, touched off by the woman whom he had shunted aside, the sight of whom—amplified by his imaginings—had turned now to obsession. He had seen her again at midday and thought about the white flesh beneath the nearly transparent silk dress caressed by a breeze.

A rare silence lay upon the house. Fu-chun and Jiao-ma had gone to the city to buy fabric; they would be away for some time. The children, Zhu-er and Ju-er, had gone to First Lord's house; they had started to do this more and more often now that Gan-er no longer played much with them.

It was an odd moment, an odd feeling. Second Lord was in the throes of an impulse as irresistible as it was indefinable. Irresistible it certainly was. Indefinable? No, not true. He knew perfectly well what this feeling was, having felt it so often in former days—in fact, each time the house happened to be empty. Something deep down surged up, inflaming a tyrannical power—the urge to subject someone to his appetites. What was aroused was not merely lusting but predatory. To take someone by complete surprise, brutally. Now *there* was excitement! It was nothing like making love, when everything was expected, everything was mutual, and in the end everything was so tiresome. This was not like that. You thrilled at the feel of your prey squirming beneath you. She would only partly resist, so inculcated in her was the authority of the power mastering her. You would sense her growing resignation, start ripping off her clothes in patches and savoring each piece of flesh as it was exposed, drunk from the cries of terror produced by the merciless blows, cries that slowly turned into panting submission. He would not stop until the groans had quieted, for they only heightened the pleasure, just as they had when as a child he'd tortured some small creature until the last spasm.

"Oh, the pleasure of rape. Who is more acquainted with it than I?"

Second Lord began to scour his memory for exploits from long ago. He recounted quickly the large number of them before his marriage. Between marrying Lady Ying and Lady Fu-chun, he had had the chance to get his claws on Tian-ma, the servant girl. Now quite advanced in age, she still worked for First Lord. When Lady Fu-chun was pregnant, he had done it to the young *ya-tou*—he couldn't recall her name now—who had ended up in a brothel. What about the second concubine? Had he not married her after raping her? No, he had not taken her by force. He was a man of breeding. He would never have married a woman he had done that to. And it was not permissible to rape a woman he had married! The whole notion was absurd. Nonetheless, this time he would have to use drastic means. He knew it would be difficult—to bond again with a woman abandoned a long time ago, during which time his own authority had been emptied of substance. It would be necessary to beat down the arrogance of the woman.

She who thought of herself as so elegant and well bred, who

never had any pleasure from me, how will she judge me from on high now? Like a tortoise—a toad? We'll see about that! Me, weaker? I'll rise up to my fullness with my chest and with my arms.

"Lao Sun!"

No response. The man was probably stealing a quick nap. Second Lord called his servant's name again, louder. Lao Sun came running, rubbing his eyes. So he had been napping. If Lao Sun was there, it meant Lady Ying had not gone out.

"I am tired of sitting. Take me to the bed so that I can sleep for a while."

Lao Sun pushed the chair to the edge of the bed, then gently took his master by the arms, placed him on the bed, and helped prop him up against the pillows.

"May Second Lord sleep well. Does Second Lord require anything else?"

"Pour me a glass of cold tea. My mouth is dry."

The sound of tea being drunk in small gulps made Lao Sun thirsty. He repressed a yawn and waited for his master to finish. Then he set the glass back on the table.

"Does Second Lord desire anything else?"

"No, nothing else."

Lao Sun was almost out the door when Second Lord spoke again. "Inform Lady Ying that I wish to see her. I have some free time today, and I would like to take advantage of it to tell her something."

As soon as Lao Sun had left, Second Lord began to tremble. His head throbbed, and his heart felt as if it would break out of his chest. After what seemed an interminable time, he heard knocking at the door. Before he could answer, the door opened gently and revealed the face of the one that he had lately been trying in vain to see from up close. She neared. In the center of the room, heavy with the sweet and unmistakable stench of opium, this unmoving presence so intimidating to him was suddenly also so reassuring. For he could tell that she, too, was intimidated. He sensed that he would be able to master her. He threw himself into a loud coughing fit as a distraction.

"Is Second Lord doing well?"

"One cannot say that I am doing well. Back pains."

Despite her reticence, Lady Ying felt obligated to maintain the role of wife. She approached and helped him to turn over.

"Let me pound you on the back," she said, sitting down on the edge of the bed. She began striking his back with regular blows.

"Ah! Ah! Uh! Uh!"

"Is there something Second Lord wishes to tell me?" she asked, not interrupting her treatment.

"Oh, yes. Don't stop. Don't stop. Feels good."

He started to cough again. His breathing grew quicker. Seizing one of his wife's hands, he placed it upon the moist skin of his chest.

"Ah! Ah! Oh, how good that feels!"

His breath reeked.

"Is there . . . something Second Lord wishes to say to me?"

"Nothing special. Just talk for a while."

He placed his right hand on his wife's thigh and started to caress it.

"What are you doing?"

"Nothing. Just being playful. Ha, ha!"

But Second Lord had no acquaintance with the honeyed language of persuasion. Suddenly his voice hardened. "Come!"

Grabbing her dress with both hands, he pulled her violently toward him. His face was beaded with sweat; his breathing was ragged.

"Second Lord . . . is unwell. I will bring him tea."

She rose so abruptly that he had no time to let go of his hold and was pulled to the floor.

"Eeaaah!"

"Second Lord has injured himself!"

Lady Ying helped him back onto the bed and propped him against the pillows. She dabbed at his forehead with a handkerchief. Exhausted and haggard, Second Lord ignored her; he could focus on nothing but the pains racking him. He struggled for breath. Gradually his breathing slowed.

"Second Lord must rest quietly. Lady Fu-chun will be back soon."

And with that, the object of his desire vanished like a ghost, leaving behind only the trace of her perfume. His eyes bulging, he reached up and gripped the bed curtains, pulling at them in rage. "Fu-chun! Come now! Faster!"

Thirteen

IT WAS STILL AFTERNOON. THE AIR WAS HEAVY WITH THE freshness leaves give off after a downpour. A ray of light pierced the curtain and floated into the middle of the room. Seemingly not looking for anything in particular to illuminate, it had lightness of an *aspara*—a heavenly flying creature—which, with its wings folded, allows itself to be carried along by a breeze. A magpie smoothed its feathers outside on the window ledge. Its periodic cry intensified the silence inside the room, in which only the thin line of blue smoke rising from the incense burner teased human thought.

Lan-ying rose from her bed and with an automatic gesture refastened her hair into a bun. She walked to the table, poured a glass of tea, and drank it in gulps. Then she sat down at the little worktable and picked up the embroidery she was doing on a pillowcase. Sitting at the window, she began work. The ray of light warmed her temples and lit up the fabric stretched on a small wooden frame, highlighting a pair of mandarin ducks, one of which was finished, the other barely outlined. Elsewhere she would probably add some roses, or perhaps some plants that suggested the proximity of water. This was her way of expressing herself, discreetly but freely. The room was her universe; apart from Xiao-fang, no one disturbed her here, no one came to ask what she was doing. Embroidering a pair of mandarin ducks on a pillowcase—was that something someone of her age ought to be doing? Was it not daring, even scandalous? She didn't think much about that anymore. She had started the project spontaneously one day and thrown herself into it. However, it didn't distract her from a question that had been gnawing at her, all the more so after what had taken place in Second Lord's chamber. She spoke out loud.

"Dao-sheng, sit. Let's talk for a little while. So rarely do we have the chance to talk, though in all the haste of our meetings nothing essential has been lost. There are so many things left unspoken. Will this life give us enough time? Let's talk, slowly and calmly. We have waited so long that we have come to know the virtue of patience. First, let the spring breezes, which soak up the rains, also dry our tears. Then the summer sun, which brings everything to fruition, will set free our dreams, frozen in the long night of waiting. Real treasures are delicate and hidden. The heart of a woman has the richness and depth of a garden. To reach its deepest part you have to follow a meandering path and come to the end of lush and secret thickets. On one side is a pond with water lilies. Lotus leaves shelter it. Sit next to this pool of water and listen to what it is telling you. Heed the heart beating there. Swollen from dew, the flower petals form a gesture of welcome. If they open too far, they risk falling off. Know how to capture not only the beauty of the surface but the beauty that springs from the roots and the desire of beauty that follows soon after. Most of all, there is the water itself. Ordinary, yet it holds the whole sky. The moon is always reflected there, and is always renewed there. The clouds float on it into infinity.

"Dao-sheng, you are a soothsayer, a doctor. You have traveled the world. You know so many things. Can you also understand that a woman carries within her that small thing that, for her, means everything?

"Other men love women solely for their flesh. Women have but one flesh, yet they have a heart as well. They have but one heart, yet they have a soul as well. Do you believe in the soul? If I were old and had lost all my beauty, would you still have braved all those dangers to find me again? Had the bandits disfigured me when I was their hostage, would you still have talked about eternity? Since someday I will be so, perhaps it would be better to hold forever to the memory of these moments of purity when your fingers felt my pulse, and to the unbreakable happiness that comes of exchanging looks and smiles. Perhaps we have rediscovered each other too late. Perhaps we should wait for another life to start over—a different life, one unburdened by all those lost years. I wonder, do you believe in another life?"

These were words Lan-ying had not yet been able to offer Dao-sheng. Even had she had that chance, she wondered, would he have been able to understand them, to hear that different voice that comes from women?

In any event, Dao-sheng will soon hear another kind of voice, one from elsewhere, and it will happen in a most unexpected manner. That tends to be how certain words reach the ears of men.

That day, a stiff breeze had made working difficult. Dao-sheng was getting ready to fold up his stand when he saw someone approaching him. It was the owner of the large inn at the Southern Gate of the city, the very one where he had had his fight with Second Lord Zhao. The innkeeper told Dao-sheng that for nearly a year he had had two strangers from far away lodging with him. These men were truly strangers. They had things like mechanical timekeepers, music boxes, and colored pictures showing human figures that were diabolical in appearance. They made themselves available to all visitors and welcomed, day or night, any who came to see them—and many did: Ordinary people drawn by curiosity and educated men seeking to engage the strangers in long discussions. That seemed to be what the two strangers were seeking, in fact. They never said no. In the end they grew very tired and so pale as to be worrisome. One of the two, the one who spoke the language well, fell ill—gravely ill, from the look of it. Doctors said that he had caught malaria.

When the innkeeper pronounced the name of the dread disease from which the stranger suffered, Dao-sheng realized why the innkeeper had sought him out. Dao-sheng had treated that disease before and word had gotten out. He had hoped to maintain discretion when it came to practicing medicine. The Great Master had taught that one heals better in the shade than out in the open. Even so, the stranger's case intrigued him.

"First I will go to the monastery, and then I will come to them," Dao-sheng said simply.

When he was brought face-to-face with the two strangers, he

remembered having spotted them once before, on the far side of the temple square, looking lost and out of place. Now here they were in the most tangible sense, yet still they seemed unreal. They had curly, light brown hair. Their beards had a reddish tint and were thick and long. The sick one was sitting up in bed, his shirt partially opened, revealing a portion of a chest thickly matted with hair. His eyes were blue-gray and deeply set. Dao-sheng wondered what feelings lay behind those eyes—what desires, what thoughts. They were not Persians and they were not Hindus. He was unsure his medicine would have any effect on these people.

"This human face, the most revealing of things, seems marked by some unfathomable mystery," he said to himself. "Let us hope that my medical arts can do something. Let's also hope that we can communicate with each other through words."

The other man, who had been sitting in a chair, rose to greet Dao-sheng. The utter strangeness of this person was accentuated by the manner in which he talked. He spoke without tones. Sometimes he mixed the tones up, the effect being simultaneously comical and touching. Likewise when he mixed up the order of words to which he lent very pedantic emphasis, as if he had learned them from some ancient book. Nonetheless, Dao-sheng was used to listening and soon managed to follow. When the sick man himself opened his mouth, Dao-sheng felt at ease, like someone lost in the forest who suddenly comes across a familiar path, for while also talking in an odd accent, the sick man spoke in a way that was almost . . . refined.

Dao-sheng examined his eyes and tongue, then took his pulse. As he had expected, he diagnosed a particularly severe form of malaria. He brought out some medications, informing the two men in great detail how to mix them and when the sick man should take them. He made clear that these were only the first course of treatment; he would have to come back in two days, and perhaps often after that, to balance the dosages against the progress of the illness.

Before he took his leave, Dao-sheng's eyes met those of the sick man. Despite the fever, which colored his pale cheeks, the man tried to smile, as if to show that he trusted Dao-sheng. Encouraged, Dao-sheng gave in to the desire to ask the questions burning on his lips.

"Where are you from?"

"We are from what they call the Ocean of the West."

"That is far from here, is it not? Do you know the distance?"

"Thousands upon thousands of *li*."

"Thousands of *li!* How long did it take you to get here?"

"We had to cross lands and oceans and overcome a thousand obstacles and dangers. It required two years in total, including a stop in the intervening countries of the South."

With that, he asked his companion to hand him a parchment scroll, sitting on a shelf on which glittered other rare-looking objects. He unrolled it and presented Dao-sheng with a map of the terrestrial world, then pointed to where they were on it.

Though the map revealed an endless landscape of the sort to which the Chinese eye was accustomed, Dao-sheng was stunned by what he was being shown. "Ah! Is the world truly as vast as this tells me? I had thought that the Empire was located in the middle, and that all other lands surrounded it. This seems to reveal that it occupies but one small corner. Are you sure that is the case?"

"We are sure, for we have traveled the path to it. However, this is not simply a small corner but quite vast enough. Is it not good that there are different lands and different peoples? It speaks of the richness of this earth."

"That is so."

Traveler that he was, and loving nothing so much as the discovery of new things, Dao-sheng felt in complete agreement with this man. His curiosity was aroused by the objects on the shelf.

Aided by his companion, who held out the objects, the sick man roused himself and explained how a prism diffracts light into all the different colors, and how a clock indicates the passing of hours and minutes by ticking and making musical tones.

Dao-sheng marveled at these things, making cries of delight and admiration that instantly transformed the sober atmosphere in the room.

"So it is in order to sell these magical objects that you have traveled so far?"

"We are not merchants. We are men of religion."

"Ah, priests. You are Buddhists?"

"No, not Buddhist. There are also different religions in the world."

"What is your religion?"

"We believe in the Lord God who created the earth."

"And what else?"

"Believing in Him, and in His Name, we are here to announce the Good News."

"What good news?"

"The Good News that a savior has come and—"

"What savior is that?"

Here the man paused. He slightly regretted having let himself get carried away. Up to this point he had endeavored to employ a more gradual approach to making his affirmations. Direct discourse could easily go astray, even create obstacles, and circumstances did not permit a full explanation. But given the intense expression of this doctor, and pushed by a disease whose outcome was uncertain, he decided to press ahead.

"Yes, a savior. None other than the Son of the Lord God, sent to earth to be our Savior. If we believe in Him, we are saved."

"Saved? That *is* news. At the moment the empire of the Mings is falling apart, and the country overrun by thieves and brigands. The power of the Son of the Sky is reaching its end, and bearded barbarians are waiting for their moment to invade. No one can escape the numbers of fate. Being saved will be a difficult matter. Where can this son of the Lord of the Sky be found?"

"He ascended to Heaven and rejoined the Father."

"If he is in Heaven, how can he save men?"

"If we believe in Him, we can be saved and ascend like Him to Heaven."

"What you say strains belief. Tell me no more today. You are tired. After you have taken the potion, you will sweat and then find you are able to sleep a little."

Fourteen

DAO-SHENG RETURNED TWO DAYS LATER. WHEN HE SAW THAT though his fever had gone down, the sick stranger's condition was still precarious, he was filled with concern. He prescribed some particularly precious herbs from his limited supply. It was important that he save the life of this man, if only in the name of hospitality. He had come from so far, from a place that was "beyond the sky." Moreover, he had come in order to say something, and had not yet managed to say it. The least of all politeness would be to allow him to say all that he had to say.

Once the consultation was at an end, during a moment of silence, Dao-sheng was again drawn in by the pale glimmer in those gray-blue eyes.

"Given that the son of your Lord of the Heavens is a savior, why does he not save you?"

"What He saves in each one of us is the soul."

"What is the soul?"

"In your heart you know what it is. Do not the Taoists speak of a soul? The Buddhists even more so? They believe that the soul is everlasting. . . ."

"The Taoists believe that the soul never dies because after death the soul is sent back along the Way. As the Way goes on forever, the soul does as well. Still, everyone dies."

"The Buddhists also believe in reincarnation. We, on the other hand, believe that the essence of every individual is his soul, and that this soul is not subordinate to the body. The body must die, but the soul cannot. The soul continues to live and lives forever aware of itself."

"If that is so, then why even bother with the body and with death? Why not simply give life to the soul?"

The question made the stranger pause for a minute. Then he replied. "That is because of Original Sin."

"Original sin?"

The stranger hesitated yet again.

"It is a complex issue that cannot be explained today in a few words. The essential for us is to affirm that the body dies and the soul does not. It lives for eternity. That is why I say that what the Savior saves is the soul, which ascends to Heaven. As for the poor body, it must endure that which the earth endures. For example, I am sick and it is possible that I will die. If I perish here, I will be buried here."

"Let us not speak of such things. You are not going to die just yet. And how sad to be buried far from your native land."

"We do not see it that way. We love human beings, not land. Our native land is wherever there are people we love. Since we are on that subject, let's put things more clearly: It is because of love that we do not die, for it is through love that we are saved."

"These are very odd thoughts, yet somehow I understand

them better. How is it you are sure that because of love we do not die?"

"It is because our Lord is love. If we believe in Him and love as He does, we will not die."

Dao-sheng could think of no response. He advised the stranger to rest, for he could see that the poor man was grimacing in pain, and that the fever was rising. He also half-wondered whether having pushed his patient to utter such outlandish things would not have led to delirium.

Nonetheless, the next time he came, unable to stop himself, Dao-sheng returned to the subject.

"Why are you always speaking of 'love' and of 'loving oneself'? It is true that our wise men use similar expressions, such as *jian-ai,* or 'love for everything,' and *fan-ai,* or 'universal love.' These are intended to create harmony in society. In private, among individuals, one does not say things such as 'Love oneself.' Instead we say, 'Take pleasure.'"

"Yes, but that is not the same thing. 'Take pleasure' one does for oneself—when something is enjoyable. 'Loving oneself' refers to something greater. You love even if there are insurmountable objects or nothing to be gained from it."

"There is truth in what you are saying—at least a truth that I understand well. I am a vagabond, a voyager, and yet I have found love. I know something about it. Anyway, you argue that the Lord of Heaven is love. What proof do you have?"

"We have proof. We believe in the Lord of Hosts, and also in His Son. He lived upon the earth. For His entire life, He did nothing but love."

"And afterward?"

"He was nailed to a cross made of wood."

"Nailed to a piece of wood? While alive? For what reason?"

"Because men are sinful and not able to recognize His love."

"And afterward?"

"Afterward, He died . . ."

"So you see? He died."

"I did not finish. I wanted to say that three days after He died, He was resurrected."

"What do you mean 'resurrected'?"

"What it means. He came back to life."

"You cannot come back to life three days after your death. For as long as I have practiced medicine I have never seen such a thing. What proof do you have of this?"

"There were witnesses."

"Where are they now?"

"They are no longer of the world. They rose to Heaven. They are in paradise."

"Ah, they are no longer of this world. This place you call paradise. Is there evidence of its existence?"

"Our holy book mentions it. Our Savior did as well. One cannot always ask for tangible evidence. There are things that are invisible to the eye. Things that we can grasp only through the spirit and with the heart."

"Again you have said something interesting, but also hard to believe."

When Dao-sheng returned for the fourth time, he found the sick stranger sitting in the chair. His patient was clearly prepared to restart their discussion. There was more color in his cheeks, and his beard was combed. Dao-sheng could see that the disease had not disappeared but that the man's body was gaining dominance over it.

This man cares little about his body, thought Dao-sheng. He has already started to receive visitors again. Some were waiting in the room next door. His energy is focused upon what he carries within him—his beliefs. His entire person, his angular body and his sharp eye, bespeak his ardor to preach, to convince, and to explain. We are shaped by what we believe and by what we hold to. This stranger has gone so far with his ideas that the day will come when he will die here, in this city where he knows no one, and in this room where he has already nearly lost his life. Are we not pushed by the same forces, Lan-ying and I—forces stronger than we are? Does what we believe have foundation? That is what I would like to hear from this man, not his belief in incredible things. Why does he not simply talk of love, a subject that would reach me?

The patient seemed to have guessed what his doctor was thinking. He went directly to the subject. "Master Dao-sheng, you are truly an eminent man. Not only do you possess the skill to heal the body but you are drawn to life's essentials. You force me to reflect deeply, you know. As we do not have much time today, let us not talk of the Lord of Heaven or of His Son. We will talk about you. You have told me that you know what it means to love. Is this not right?"

"It is. I love someone. I am not able to tell you who. But I love this person from the bottom of my heart. To distraction. There can be no doubt of this."

"From the bottom of your heart and to distraction, you say.

Do you mean by this that you love this person more than yourself?"

"That is beyond question."

"We are therefore forced to concede that if we truly love, the love we feel is greater than ourselves. That it surpasses us. For if one loves truly, one enters into another realm, and in this realm, without forgetting that we are mortal, we believe that while we might die, the love we feel within us will not. So much so that we say to those we love, 'You will not die!' The truer our love—for there are different levels of love—the more we swear that it is eternal. The Chinese say that their love is 'more enduring than Heaven and Earth' or that they will love 'until the mountains melt and the oceans run dry.'

"My good friend Dao-sheng, do you not hear throughout the world all the voices ring out exclaiming, 'Love never dies! You will never die!' And all these voices join to form one enormous path. Yes, *the* Way—the Tao. I believe it no coincidence that in Chinese *Tao* has a double meaning: both 'way' and 'word,' both 'walking' and 'speaking.' Can we not see that by walking and by speaking, all those loved beings in the world form an immense Way that exalts true life and triumphs over death? One thing above all do I want to tell you now: To form the Way to true life, love must begin with a promise. It must begin with some-one saying, right from the start, as best as we can conceive of it, 'I love you, and you will not die.'"

The stranger paused for breath. His eyes shone with an ardent light. It was clear that he was, almost to his own astonishment, inspired.

Alone again, Dao-sheng immediately pushed his thoughts further:

This man who left everything behind to come here must be crazy. Living as he does requires a touch of madness. Of course there are any number of Taoists and Buddhists who remove themselves from the world by going to monasteries and retreating into the mountains. Yet they lead quiet lives. This man is not content to do that; indeed, he puts his very life at risk. Nothing else matters. The other thing about this man: If he abandoned everything to live simply and to do as he pleased, there would be nothing further to say. However, because he swears by love, he is forced to plunge headfirst into the world. Taoists talk of accepting the universe of the living. The Buddhists speak of compassion and charity. With his stories of love, this man is forced into action: to act, to persuade, to wait, to hope—in short, to feel passion, as a man driven mad would feel passion. Perhaps I am the same. To feel as I do, to risk what I have, to live on the run—this also requires a touch of madness. We are madmen, he and I, madmen incapable of violence and capable only of speaking of love. Yet there is a difference between us. He loves all creatures in the world, and relies entirely upon his Lord of Heaven. I love a woman whom I cannot have. Which of us is stranger?

Fifteen

"UNTIL THE MOUNTAINS MELT AND THE OCEANS RUN DRY. More enduring than Heaven and Earth." That was something one could say only once in one's life, and each of us was put into the world to say it. What the stranger said must be true: Once you have said this to your beloved, she will not die, and you can look back at your life without regret. Even when lovers see each other for an instant each day, and during this instant can neither touch nor speak. Yes, one might think oneself happy, if one can arrive at happiness by relying upon the divine breath of the *shen,* to pronounce these words that for all eternity have been waiting to be spoken.

Thus Dao-sheng pursued his inner monologue one summer night while in his tiny room at the monastery. The air retained the heat of the day until after midnight. Through the open shutter, he could see the Milky Way sending its starry waves rolling across the sky. The infinite universe offers a spectacle simultaneously grand and poignant, in which thousands of beings are caught up endlessly spinning in a gigantic motion.

Who wouldn't feel crushed and lost in the face of this? Though we strain to see, yet we can make out each point of light along the length of this dazzling cloth. Each burns with its own flame, without pretension and without pomp. Each burns while offering a sign to the others, who burn just like it, and together they form an unbreakable bond. Star to star, heart to heart. These stars were no different from those living on earth. Or was it that those on earth modeled themselves on the stars? As a soothsayer, Dao-sheng knew well the intimate connections between the twenty-eight celestial houses and the fates of men. Until now, this had been abstract knowledge. Now, caught up in this nocturnal mystery, he was shaken by what this circular motion revealed to him, endlessly renewing the universal flame. Each one reaches his own inescapable end.

Following that night, Dao-sheng decided to alter his habit of sleeping. He would refuse to allow himself to fall victim— stretched out on the bed and coiled up in his blanket—to a restless sleep invaded by nightmares and troubled thoughts. He discovered the advantages of sleeping sitting up, supported by a folded pillow. It was more peaceful, more pure. Content to watch the skies, cloudy or star-filled, he was less bothered when sleep was slow in coming.

Or he had conversations with Lan-ying, something he could scarcely do during the day. These imaginary conversations were a comfort to him; they made the days seem less long, and all the waiting more tolerable. Propped up, at ease, he closed his eyes. That was when he saw Lan-ying approach, take his hand, and this time care for him as if he were the patient.

How great was the change that had come over him. Forced by the power of events into becoming a fugitive, he had always resisted excessive discipline. Even his time among the Taoists had not altered his ways. Haunted by longing and nostalgia, he had wandered the world until the day he realized that their source was connected to the very thread of his life. So he had responded, and here he was, now, in this place, in a state of voluntary passivity, a tree rooted in the soil of the heart, patiently extending its branches and spreading its leaves to collect love's gifts: Light, breezes, dew, cleansing thunder, and welcome rain.

With the advent of the Festival of the Double Seven, Dao-sheng started to observe the two stars, the Herdsman and the Weaver, on opposite ends of the Milky Way. During the deepest part of the night, you could barely see them so brightly did they sparkle. He was suddenly ashamed that he not seen them before, these lovers who were born at the same moment as the Heaven and the Earth and who endure as long as they do. It is said that by celestial decree they are permitted to meet once a year, and that on the seventh day of the seventh month—the appointed day of their meeting—the magpies are responsible for building a bridge across the Milky Way, that the lovers might cross to each other.

Here was the perfect parallel for himself and Lan-ying. They were more fortunate than these stars, of course, for they could see each other nearly every day. Still, the sense of the drama was so similar: To get so close without being able to touch. Dao-sheng wondered whether he had instinctively avoided observing these stars for fear of finding in them a tragic reaffirmation of his and Lan-ying's situation.

The night of the festival arrived, and he had decided to watch the stars along with everyone else. At a precise moment after midnight, surrounded by mists, the light from the Milky Way became diffused. Immersed in this sidereal haze, the stars were approaching each other. To wonder whether this was real or imagined was pointless. In this mythic night, all the lovers below the Heavens, with tightness in their hearts and their eyes brimming with tears, watched the sacred event. They whispered their pledges, for inhibitions disappear in darkness. Life is lived on a word, a word that nothing in the world can stop from climbing up to the sky, reaching even to the *shen*. Their destiny will be their own, however dire that destiny might be. What human passion would dare such a joining, once a year for all eternity?

There the two stars were, in the heat of deepest night, their white fires merging, enfolding each other in an act of even greater clarity. Dao-sheng felt physical desire surge up from within. His body swelled to it and grew, opening to the other body in his dreams, which opened itself in return. He explored this body, softening to its touch, down to its bones, penetrating through its points of vulnerability, melting into it and dissolving into the ecstatic memory of the milky Origins.

One day, toward the end of the seventh month, when Lan-ying and Xiao-fang greeted him as they came out of the temple, Dao-sheng, impelled by some unseen force, calmly and without raising his voice, said quickly but clearly, "On the third watch of the Festival of the Moon. At the back gate."

Stunned by his own audacity, he immediately regretted having spoken. What would come of this?

In the days leading up to the Moon Festival, which occurs on the fifteenth day of the eighth month, Dao-sheng struggled to maintain his composure. As before, he accompanied the one-legged beggar to the midday food distribution. He looked closely but discreetly at Lan-ying, trying but failing to read her eyes and lips. Was her expression simply closed to him? Or was it something even more complex? He found it worrisome that Lan-ying no longer came to the temple.

A woman's heart is a difficult thing to read, he reflected in his pain. However profound the love between a man and a woman, a simple misunderstanding can cause irreparable damage. I wonder if I shocked Lan-ying. Perhaps she never envisioned such an adulterous meeting. The worst would be if she thought my intentions were base.

Dao-sheng's anxiety was approaching despair when Lao Sun came to announce to the Great Monk, and through him to the poor, that Lady Ying would be suspending the food distribution for a time, given the imminence of the Moon Festival. To celebrate the festival, families would prepare cakes and other foods for a nightlong outdoor vigil. No seeker of food would have trouble finding it. Dao-sheng couldn't help wondering whether Lan-ying would see him again.

The Festival of the Moon. Sometime around the second watch. In the city and villages, people were enjoying their reunions—symbolized by the roundness of the full moon. Sitting in circles in courtyards or on terraces, they recounted legends and sang the ancient songs; voices and laughter rang out in the night, as rich as the delicacies upon which they feasted. The earth was so brightly lit that lanterns were superfluous.

During his life on the road, Dao-sheng had often walked all night, yet on this evening he felt a loneliness such as he had never before known. He had taken the path to the Zhao estate and now found himself standing before the back gate. It was just before the time of the third watch. He went a little further along the path and hid among the tall grass growing next to the wall. He thought he heard the sounds of human voices, but they were instantly drowned out by the deafening drone of insects. He lifted only his head and was startled by the size of the moon. Floating in the sky, making a perfect ring in the heart of the celestial vault, it seemed to crystallize all the waiting done by all living creatures, who at this very hour were bathed in its unreal and sacred light, murmuring their reply. Such universal communion made Dao-sheng feel even more alone. Would she come?

He waited, getting gradually better at distinguishing between sounds. He could hear the beating of his own heart, and the croaking of frogs from inside the garden. He was suddenly struck by the thought that he would never know what it would be like to enter the garden, or to sit next to Lan-ying and admire the lotus flowers blossoming on the pond. Carried on a note of despair, or some other source, a prayer came to him. "Let me come into your garden like a ray of moonlight that illuminates everything but disturbs nothing. Let it reveal all creatures living there, yet allow every sound and smell to be guided by its own nature, in all its innocence. O woman who has been mocked by corrupt desires, who has sought to lift me toward pure trust and airy lightness, I understand your long-ing. You have gone so far. Perhaps too far for me. But believe that I will follow you. I have the patience necessary. Eternity is not too long until we will be together. Step by step will I catch up to you."

A creaking sound tore the night air, as if made by giant shears. It both startled Dao-sheng and was familiar to him. In fact it gave him a shudder of joy, for he heard it every day at noon. It was the noise of a heavy wooden gate being opened. Someone was there. Dao-sheng remained motionless, holding his breath. Then he saw the outline of Xiao-fang. He leapt up and ran toward her. She shushed him, then said in a low voice, "Everyone is still awake. Luckily they are all gathered at the front gate. The children are at First Lord's. Please, we must be careful and cannot stay for long."

Lan-ying hung back. She was trembling. She had come to this rendezvous with her whole heart, but something reminded her that she was committing a bold act of rebellion, or at least one that was compromising. She lingered in the garden, trying desperately not to think about this, instead willing herself to become absorbed in the moment, a moment that had instanta-neously thrust her deep into the past. This smell of dew-covered grass that enveloped her in its silken shawl, the song of longing with which all of nature lullabies itself, and most of all this celestial display of jades and diamonds beyond counting— all this she remembered. Her most secret life was connected to the moon, which had accompanied her when she was a young maid and had gone to the village to see a theatrical perfor-mance. It was her most trusted confidante later, when she was tormented by sleeplessness. And when she was freed from the kidnappers. On the road home her heart had nearly broken at the universe's splendor, and at the thought that amid such splendor man could be capable of violence.

In its rare instants of pure dream, a woman's secret life is nourished by the moon. After all, the moon is inhabited by the goddess Chang-e, whose loving heart illuminates it night after night. She derives power from weakness, from a humility wrought of receptive emptiness, capable of carrying another life and, once life is there, of reflecting a light that comes from far away—having passed through her, it neither blinds nor harms. That is why in the shadows she offers consolation. She soothes with her living rhythm the song of the sea and of the blood; she softens with dew the fever of the soil and of the plants.

Lan-ying approached the gate, a lotus flower in its final and most glorious autumn flowering. In the face of her singularity, Dao-sheng remained an observer. He felt the gratitude the earth feels when it receives purifying water. Wordlessly, with a lump in his throat, he took a step forward, then stopped. The initiative needed to come from the woman. After a moment's hesitation, she extended her right hand.

Dao-sheng joined it in his. "Lan-ying," he said simply.

Her reply was inaudible; only from the movement of her lips would one have guessed that Dao-sheng's name was being pronounced. There followed a silence that she broke by putting her left hand on the back of his hand; he responded with the same gesture. So were their four hands superimposed, imprinting their harmonious breathing. This was what these two beings wanted to do in each other's presence; this was what they could do. They renewed what they had done on the edge of the bed, the memory of which had followed them, leaving them with a thirst that they had thought unquenchable.

This time they were standing; their intermingling was thus even more complete. Hands as soft and as smooth as jade covered hands as rough as a gnarled tree. Vein to vein, fiber to fiber, leaf to leaf, branch to branch, what started in the fingertips and in the palms was carried by the meridians to all parts of the body. Immersed in the rhythmic waves that came from them and also carried them, the lovers floated into their own world.

Could they do more on this night of the full moon, which symbolized the joy of their reunion? Before their meeting their thoughts had been unformulated or unacknowledged. Dao-sheng might have hoped, in a moment of outrageous boldness, for some further intimacy. But all this vague desire had evaporated. In the current state of their feelings, marked by millenarian modesty and distant hope, bringing their bodies closer was not yet possible. More urgent and more intense than an embrace was the look they could offer each other in this small corner of the earth, in this brief moment under the skies. This look was the most precious of gifts, permitting them to hold and then to relive, again and again, freely and without constraint, the presence of the other.

As amazing as it might seem, other than furtively or from a distance, they had never really been able to gaze at each other—unhurriedly, fearlessly, unrestrainedly—from close up, with full hearts, leisurely taking in the emanation of the soul, lit up by the eyes, caressing the greatest enigma of all, which is the human face. It is through our faces that we recognize and love one another. The one of whom he had dreamed for a lifetime was finally before him, rendered with even greater poignancy and purified by the nocturnal clarity.

Dao-sheng's face, too, felt cleansed. Gone was the slightly drawn expression, that mixture of complacency and suffering; gone as well was that look of feigned interest that his profession required. All that remained in its lines was what he felt for his beloved, as she truly was.

Melancholy had vanished from Lan-ying's expression, replaced by luminous simplicity. The wrinkles and the hint of silver in her hair were but signs of an untainted dream. Her eyebrows, eyes, lips, crowning the contours of her face, were transformed into a unique treasure, a star among stars, except that she was not distant but present in body and in soul. Their dazzled eyes could see no more. The moment of magic was condensed into two suspended pearls against a backdrop of blue satin.

Already time was growing short. Those gathered in the courtyard would soon be dispersing. Someone might come into the garden. It was the moment for words. Certain vital things needed to be said—the most important thing we can do in this world—and the rest would follow. Dao-sheng had not forgotten the words echoing in his spirit. "Mountains melt and oceans run dry. More enduring than Heaven and Earth." Yet, somehow, at this late hour, when nature's ten thousand sounds had suddenly gone quiet, these edifying phrases didn't spring to his lips. Instead, he found simple words that came from the heart, the same words they had exchanged when he had been in Lan-ying's room.

"We must thank Heaven and Earth that we have been united at last," said Dao-sheng.

"Yes."

"We are together again. Never to part."

"Yes."

Bolder than she had been that first time, Lan-ying ventured, "We will never be parted now. In this life, even in the next life, we will always be together."

Sixteen

AS LAO SUN HAD PREDICTED, ZHU THE SIXTH'S WAYS CAUGHT
up with him. Lao Sun had envied this inveterate womanizer,
who had served many masters and secretly led a dissipated life,
yet he knew he was not at all like him. Lao Sun would never
have dared to go to the city every night with money jingling in
his pocket to play games and drink. He would never have
dared pay for women. And take advantage of Lady Fu-chun
herself! He found it hard even to imagine such a thing! Most
incredibly, Zhu the Sixth had tried to blackmail Lady Fu-chun,
asking for large sums of money to replace what he had lost at
dice. Unnerved by such boldness, she had found a way to
remove him from the household, indeed from the entire
region.

Well, such was the world. Zhu the Sixth had chased women
and had had more than he could count. He, Lao Sun, had
loved only one woman, and loved her still. It was bad luck that
she ended up in a brothel. As he had explained to Zhu, he had
only just arrived at the Zhao household when Second Lord

violated Shun-zi and then sold her off, breaking his heart. He kept his secret as carefully as he hoarded his savings, hidden between the bricks in a wall. He would never forget her. Though she was now a prostitute, in his mind she kept her girlish innocence. Zhu the Sixth had urged him to go and visit her. He had not. As he was leaving, his womanizing friend had winked at him, as if to say, "No one's watching you now, my honest old chum. Go and get her!" Easy to say.

One day, however, Lao Sun left the house by the back gate. Dressed in clean clothes, wearing a small round hat Second Lord had given him at the time of his nuptials with Lady Fu-chun, he might have passed for a traveling merchant, so long as he didn't open his mouth. He walked briskly in the direction of the city, crossed the river to the side where the docks were located, and entered a part of town where he had never ventured before. Once there, he felt like an inexperienced swimmer who finds himself in deep water and panics. This was the pleasure side of town, crammed with inns, opium houses, and shady hotels. So murky was the atmosphere that it seemed to suffocate you.

Asking directions to the brothel was out of the question. Lao Sun would sooner have died. He took his time locating on his own the place he sought, thanks to a description Zhu the Sixth had given him. Connecting two streets was a short alley, in the middle of which stood a building with a door painted black. Over the door was hung an enormous red lantern. Lao Sun did not approach the place directly; like a crab he zigzagged his way there. Finally, however, he found himself at the corner of the street and the alley, near the black door, trying hard to look as if he just happened to be passing by. Unfortunately, few people were about at this hour of the afternoon, and Lao Sun's neat clothes and new hat made him stand out. He moved away, then returned when he saw a man go down the alley, push open the door, and slip inside with the agility of a cat.

That decided it. He made another approach. Standing before the black door, Lao Sun heard from within the shrill voices of women, interspersed with laughter. His legs buckled; he had barely strength enough to make it back to the far end of the alley. There he caught his breath and began to berate himself.

"It's not as if I've come to do something shameful. All I want is to see Shun-zi!"

Back to the black door. This time he would do it. Things looked favorable. The door was ajar; all he had to do was push it. A woman of a certain age stuck out her head to see who was there. Her jowly face melted into a honeyed smile when she saw Lao Sun.

"Come in, good sir! Please, come in!"

In response, all Lao Sun could manage was to mumble his thanks and remove his hat. Lowering his head, he went through the doorway.

"Is this sir's first time?"

The woman's voice was reassuring.

In a large room that evidently served as both a sitting room and a bar, she addressed him again. "Here every client finds what he wants. We have superb girls. The others aren't too bad either. The choice is yours. Please, sit."

"Superb or not bad, I don't care. I have come to see Shun-zi."

Lao Sun's heavy accent made it clear to the madam that she was dealing with a peasant.

"Ah, Shun-zi. Does sir know her, then?"

"A long time ago . . ."

"I shall call her right away. She will serve you well. She knows how!"

These words made Lao Sun blush to his ears. While the woman was absent, instead of sitting as she had invited him to do, he stood awkwardly in the middle of the room, twirling his hat. He prepared himself for the shock.

It turned out to be even more brutal than he had expected. She was suddenly standing in the doorway, wearing an outrageously flowery dress. Her face was puffy and overly made up. Her lacquered hair gleamed; there were no more bangs, which used to give her a look of girlish freshness. Lao Sun struggled to see in the creature standing before him the Shun-zi of days gone by. He had nearly succeeded when from her sad face emerged a smile.

"Lao Sun! Is that you?"

"Yes. I happened to be coming into town today and thought I would stop by to say hello."

"You went to the trouble of coming all this way. Why not take advantage and spend a little time here?" asked the madam in a persuasive voice.

For all Lao Sun's inexperience, he was able to grasp what was going on. With a great surge of dignity, he forced himself to act casually and asked the price. With the hand that wasn't trembling, he took out his purse, carefully counted out the requisite number of coins, and gave them to the woman.

Preceded by Shun-zi, Lao Sun was taken into a room in which everything assaulted the senses—the hideous furniture, the prominence of the bed; everything was red, vulgar and filthy—the walls, bedcovers, screen. Even the tray of cracked lacquer on which sat some cups and a teapot was tainted by this sad-looking color, the color of clients' arteries and the hidden blood of prostitutes. One thing softened Lao Sun's heart: The light green imitation jade bracelet Shun-zi still wore. She had bought it from a peddler who stopped by the house. Lao Sun remembered this because he had been there; he had just been hired.

The room was stiflingly hot. Shun-zi helped him remove his jacket. Then, as if it were the most natural thing in the world, she directed her hands toward Lao Sun's cloth belt.

"So, Lao Sun, you wanted to come here?"

"Why are you touching my belt?"

"To undo it, of course. Otherwise how will we manage things?"

"Manage what things?"

"What a funny question. You are here and you have paid. It's what you want, isn't it?"

"Ah. Well . . . not right away. We have time."

"Not that much time. They like things to move along."

"That isn't why I came here today."

"What do you mean?"

"What do I mean? Okay, you asked. I want to buy you back."

"Buy me back? What on earth are you talking about? That would cost a fortune!"

"A fortune? I have it. I've been saving up, you know. How much?"

"Hundreds of silver ounces."

"That's . . . a lot of money. To get that much I'll need more time." Lao Sun struggled to maintain his composure, though he could feel his heart sinking, dragging down with it his self-confidence. "Believe me, Shun-zi. I'll find a way."

He didn't know what he would do but was determined he would try. Pained as he was by this ugly room, Lao Sun found Shun-zi's face even more painful and poignant. It had taken on color, re-animated by a soul that had long been absent. Already her eyes were shining in that way that had captured his heart when they had all lived together under the Zhao roof. The proverb had it right: Though a lotus flower might grow out of pond mud, nothing soils the jadelike purity of its petals.

"I didn't know there were people in the world as honest and loyal as you, Lao Sun," said Shun-zi, breaking into sobs. "If I belonged to you, I would serve you for three lifetimes!"

"One lifetime will do. I won't ask for more. I'll get you out of this place. You've said I'm loyal. Well, I *am* loyal. I'm *not* like Zhu the Sixth! I will get you out of here. You'll see!"

Shun-zi began to cry harder; tears flowed like water through broken dikes. After using no fewer than three handkerchiefs to dry them, she asked, either out of curiosity or as a distraction, "And . . . what became of Zhu the Sixth?"

"He just got himself kicked out of the Zhao house, that's what happened."

"Is this true? He was kicked out as well?"

"Yes, though for . . . for other reasons. He was something. Can you believe it? He was fooling around with Lady Fu-chun!"

"That doesn't seem possible! But then, anything can happen in this Zhao family! And after?"

"After? Well, what had to happen, happened. He was kicked out and . . . You know, it might have all gone on like that without anyone the wiser, except that Zhu the Sixth couldn't keep his mouth shut. For all his fancy manners, he was as dirty as they come. He not only chased women but drank. And he loved to gamble. In fact he lost everything in a game and then tried to blackmail Lady Fu-chun into giving him some money. Well, she set a trap for him, and he fell right into it."

"My goodness! What kind of trap?"

"First you have to know that ever since he got paralyzed, Second Lord has been grumpier than ever. Most often he sleeps alone. Lady Fu-chun has her bedroom next door. Sometimes, when Lady Fu-chun doesn't feel well herself, or the children are sick, she sleeps in their room and old Jiao-ma sleeps in her room, so that if Second Lord yells for help, she can come running. Maybe you can guess how Lady Fu-chun set her trap."

"Not completely."

"One night she arranged to meet Zhu the Sixth, except that Jiao-ma was sleeping in her bed. You can imagine what happened next. He slipped inside her room like a fish into a fishbowl and groped his way to the bed. When he started fondling the body under the covers, he began to realize something was wrong. Instead of a soft, plump body, whoever he was fondling was bony and lumpy. But he didn't stop. Then Jiao-ma screamed out, 'What's going on? Help! Help! I'm being robbed.' Lady Fu-chun came rushing in. 'Aha! It's you, Zhu the Sixth! Did you come to steal my jewels?' He was dumbstruck. Lady Fu-chun's face turned to stone. 'Now you listen to me. To insult a woman of a good family is serious. It means forced labor, or getting sent to the northern borders.' Zhu the Sixth was quick enough to grasp that being sent to the borders was a death sentence. He immediately confessed that he had come to steal the jewels.

Second Lord, who hadn't guessed the real truth, had him dragged off to the *ya-men*. The so-called thief got off with a month in prison and a light beating. He left to find work somewhere else."

"Zhu the Sixth got what he deserved. Yet in these matters the poor always lose. The rich get away with everything."

Shun-zi's reply reminded Lao Sun of the injustice she had suffered. He returned to the reason for his visit.

"The Zhao family has committed too many sins. I won't stay there for long. Wait for me!"

Seventeen

WINTER YIELDED TO AN EARLY SPRING, WHICH ESTABLISHED itself without too much backtracking. Soon it was nearly the third month of the year. In the city as in the countryside, the air was filled with a heavy blanket of fragrance from plum blossoms and flowering lilacs. Constantly called upon to wrangle with dates because of his profession, Dao-sheng was aware that he was beginning the third year of his new life in the South. He allowed himself to be carried by the flow of days. Whether they were going by too quickly or too slowly was the kind of question that no longer figured in his way of calculating the passage of time. His life had taken on a different sort of rhythm, one obedient to a hope that was beyond him. With some rare exceptions—such as when Lan-ying was too tired to distribute food, or when he was busy with a client or a patient and unable to go to the back gate at noon—he moved through each day in anticipation of her presence. Each glimpse brought its portion of joy and its element of suffering, born of the wordless brevity of their interaction. Fulfilled desire cohabited with emptiness. He could not deny that inside him stirred the same passion that stirs all nature, and that he continued to hope for more. He was tempted to ask her to do something he knew was unworthy of her—to pretend to be sick so they could enjoy more moments of intimacy. He was fully aware that Lan-ying would not lower herself to commit such an act. They had already done the most they could do during the Festival of the Moon.

Lan-ying had her own way of seeing things, her own reasons. These were to be respected. The thought calmed Dao-sheng, allowing him to sense the change that had taken place within him. Connected to the very root of his life, another self was growing unstoppably, like the trunk of an ancient pine tree that has split the rock blocking its path upward. He wondered whether this other self was still him, whether he was obedient to its laws. The answer to that question was beyond him; all he knew was that it was there. An increasing number of those who came to him for a consultation were no longer content with simple predictions; they wanted him to tell them how to live. In him they saw a man who no longer "ran after lakes and rivers," a man who had found virtue and wisdom. This was a role Dao-sheng had neither envisioned for himself nor wished to play. He was but a poor creature bound to a fate that until then had escaped his understanding.

At the outset of the Festival of *Qing-ming*, the sky had generously granted the farmers' wishes and provided plentiful rain. Mirroring the groups of clouds that passed overhead, the flooded rice paddies turned dazzling emerald green. The arrival of summer brought high hopes for a good harvest. The hearts of men brimmed with the desire for affirmation and celebration. The Festival of *Duan-wu,* or Double Five, would be a particularly joyous one. This festival occurs when the year nears its culminating point, and symbolizes humanity's attempt to make life triumphant. It falls, of all days, on the anniversary of the death of the poet Qu Yuan more than two thousand years before.

The month preceding the festival, families busily prepared foods and delicacies, notably those little cakes stuffed with salted or sugared rice wrapped in rose leaves. When steam-cooked, the cakes exuded the perfumed odor of fresh earth, giving rise in every home to a chorus of collective joy. When the day arrived, houses had been decorated with sage leaves, and over their doors hung a red sign bearing a phrase or a painted image. Sacrifices were made to the gods of the hearth and the soil at roadside shrines. The great temples overflowed with people.

That day, Lan-ying did not distribute food. Everyone, rich or poor, could find things to eat everywhere he or she turned. Early in the afternoon, accompanied by Xiao-fang, who shared her chair, and followed by Gan-er, who walked behind, she went to the temple to burn incense. After this they went to the regional capital's Western Gate, and from there to the large bridge spanning the river. It was here that the dragon-boat race would take place. Progress was painfully slow along the road, which consisted of one continuous flood of humanity. Finally, the chair was set down next to some others on the higher ground that had been reserved for the women. Men and children crammed the riverbank below them. The bridge, too, was so tightly packed with people that no one on it could move more than his head. Most wore straw hats. Seen from afar, the bridge gave the illusion of a crouching dragon whose scales fluttered in the wind.

From one of the bridge's central arches hung an enormous red-satin balloon, which glinted in the sun. This was the prize. The bridge was the finish line. Downstream, near a bend in the river some distance off, were four dragon boats covered with brightly colored streamers. While waiting for the competition to begin, people greeted one another, jostled, yelled, laughed. In the vast open air, the crowd noise was sometimes broken by the festive sound of strings of firecrackers being set off, sending up powdery puffs of smoke.

Given that the race was not yet close to starting, the men massed along the shore had plenty of time to gaze up at the higher terrain, not far from the top of the bridge. The women positioned there transformed it into a wondrous place. Their dresses were lighter, given that this was the hot season, and combined with the parasols they opened every time the sun peeked out from behind the clouds, they created a charming confusion of color and shape. Most miraculous, so far as the men were concerned, was the gathering of so many radiant female faces—right there, for all to see! It was as fascinating as a star-filled night to the men, painfully avid contemplators and yet eternal denigrators of women.

Dao-sheng was standing on the bank, his gaze similarly directed toward this mesmerizing focal point. His hand shading his eyes, he observed the women, at first casually and then with greater concentration. Suddenly he thought he could make out a light blue dress next to a purple one. These had to be Xiao-fang and Lan-ying. He lifted his arm to wave, aware of the futility of the gesture. Like everyone else, city dwellers and farmers, alike, he was wearing a short shirt of white material, and from above he would have been indistinguishable.

The crowd grew steadily more excited. On the riverbank, young people cavorted and squabbled happily. Dao-sheng could see Gan-er and the children from the Zhao family, whom he recognized from having watched them attend the school not far from the temple. He approached Gan-er and learned that Lady Fu-chun and Jiao-ma were also in attendance. Only the guards remained back at the house with Second Lord, whose illness, said Gan-er, had become more serious and forced him to stay in bed.

The sonorous clang of the gong announced that the race had begun. Two boats, their prows transformed into dragon heads held high and spitting fire, left the starting line. Gaining in brightness, their streamers fluttering in the wind, they began making their way upriver, their approach marked by the deafening noise of drums and the rhythmic chant of the rowers: *"Hang-yo! Hang-yo!"*

Standing behind the dragons' heads, red scarves wrapped around their heads, the boats' leaders urged their teams on. Naked from the waist up, covered with tattoos of scales, these men felt they truly were descendants of the original Dragon. On this special day *they* were dragons. Made drunk by that thought, each sacrificed himself to the effort, helping to unleash between waves and clouds the pulse of the great original rhythm.

Dao-sheng, who had come only to observe, felt the crowd's sway. Memories of the North surged up in him, quickening his pulse: the burst dikes, the slave laborers pitting themselves against the overwhelming power of the water, their bare torsos a pathetic defense against a force more unstoppable than a wild beast suddenly unchained. So many were carried off—so many, straws by the shovelful.

Dao-sheng guessed that most of the men on these boats did not know how to swim. Long since transformed into earth-bound peasants, these descendants of the Dragon were no longer capable of fantastic feats. Nonetheless, their fate depended equally upon the element of water. They spent the entire year in anticipation of this precious commodity, which sometimes seemed only too pleased to play the game of life and death with them. This year there had been just enough water to make the farmers happy. Any more or any less would have meant drought or floods. She had become a capricious goddess, looked upon with an equal measure of love and fear. This festival, even this race, was proof. Beginning with the death of the poet Qu Yuan in the Milo River, it had been held to show the ways in which men's lives were connected to water. Qu Yuan, the first known poet in China, a loyal servant of the regime, had been held in contempt by a corrupt ruler. While in exile he became the bard of his land. His lamentations, transmuted into a plea to the gods, were known to all. Throwing himself into the Milo River, the poet had performed a sacrificial act that renewed through water the union of the Earth and the Heavens.

The poet symbolized man's veneration of the true Way. To celebrate his memory was to celebrate the triumph of life. By eating rice cakes and fresh fish—initially intended to be tossed into the water, to appease aquatic monsters so that they might spare the body of the martyred poet—men gained new strength and confidence. These humble peasants, whose lives were dictated by the rule of others and governed by the needs of the land, and who thus were accustomed to backbreaking labor, refound their dignity. Their bulging muscles glistened. One would say that as they rowed, huffing and grunting, they had thrown off their yokes and attained a kind of ecstatic sovereignty through the intermingling of human and divine spirits. Who would not embrace these Sons of the Dragon? They would overthrow the powerful of this lower world if the latter betrayed their pact with Heaven. A harmonious life was theirs to dream. Revolt, too, lay in their hands.

Reflecting on all of this, Dao-sheng thought of his own life. The questions and turns of thought upon which his mind dwelled so often had returned. He himself had revolted once; he had broken free. After his escape he had known troubled waters, living from hand to mouth, then with the Taoist monks, though without ever surrendering his will. This period had been followed by a life of wandering, a quest that finally had come to an end and turned into a discipline—that of love. Yet even in love had he remained a rebel. Neither he nor Lan-ying had followed convention, or done anything according to common law.

She was there, blue dress against blue sky. Almost within reach—yet also distant, as if exhaled by the canopy of air. So the quest had no end; it was a fire that would burn indefinitely. That was the truth, their truth. It was happiness simply to be here, on this festival day, in this brilliant sunlight, without shadow of weariness.

He wondered if she could see him now from up there. There was no doubt she was thinking about him. That should have been enough. Under this bright sun, something had happened on the earth: Two hearts had refound each other. Anonymous though they were, these two hearts beat to the rhythm of a song more intoxicating than that emanating from this joyous throng. Dao-sheng joined his cry of exultation with theirs. He took advantage of all the noise to shout out lustily, "Lan-ying!" then experienced an incredible sense of relief. All the mumbling done under his breath had taken much out of him. He waved his arms and shouted, "Lan-ying!" over and over. No one noticed, for the crowd's roar had reached its height. One of the boats, passing the other, pushed toward the middle arch. The leader in the red scarf stretched as high as he could and touched the red balloon hanging from it.

Then, without the drums slowing, the two boats passed under the bridge and moved toward the dock that had been prepared for them. To the applause of the spectators, the rowers threw the rice cakes and fish and shrimp made of straw. The excitement remained high. Everyone was waiting for the two boats of the second race. It had begun! There came the sound of the gong. The noise of drums and chants mixed furiously together. Men will never tire of pretending that races are life-or-death struggles; it is their way of liberating themselves from fear.

After this second heat, the victors went back down the river to the starting line. It was time to run the final race.

Firecrackers made the air incandescent. The yellow-gold straw fish and shrimp covered the river's surface. Carried by the current, some reached the shore, where little children ran into the water to gather them up.

That was when the thing happened that mars every festival. In the rush to get the straw toys, a boy accidentally got shoved far out into the current headfirst, his legs in the air. It was almost comic. Then the legs disappeared below the surface. Several began to cry out, "He's drowning!" yet no one moved— apparently, no one knew how to swim. While he was taking off his shirt, Dao-sheng turned reflexively to see whether Gan-er was still there. He was gone.

Dao-sheng forged into the river. A few feet from the shore the riverbed declined sharply, and it was nearly impossible not to lose one's footing. The water was frigid; his muscles seized up. He felt around with his hands but came upon nothing.

The boy must have been further out; he was determined to look. Here was a life that needed saving, a life in the balance: The right move would restore a life; the wrong one would lose it forever. With a mighty kick of his legs, Dao-sheng pushed himself further into the current. He came across a body writhing. Reaching ahead with his arms, he pulled it toward the shore, then hauled it out of the water. The effort made his head spin. Without catching his breath, he bent over and picked the boy up by the feet and held him upside down. There was a moment—a mere blink of the eye and yet an eternity—while the water came streaming out of the boy's open mouth, which was so rigid that it reminded the spectators of that of a dead fish. Then came a sharp cry, a pathetic noise, like that of a newborn brought into the world of the living.

A number of women had come running and stopped, relieved to see that the child was not theirs. They formed a circle around Gan-er and Dao-sheng, who was the hero of the moment, mildly embarrassed by his drenched trousers and the rivulets of water streaming down his bare chest. Some handed him linen handkerchiefs. Lan-ying and Xiao-fang approached. The latter busied herself with taking off Gan-er's soaked jacket and drying him. Lan-ying gave Dao-sheng her handkerchief, which he dabbed at his shoulders and neck. It carried that perfume—that perfume he knew better than anyone. He'd once had another handkerchief that carried that scent, but he'd lost it during his escape—probably in the water. Not wanting to linger with it in front of all these people, he handed the handkerchief back to Lan-ying and received in exchange her fervent thanks, which everyone watching acknowledged with approving nods and congratulations. He was handed his shirt. At that exact moment, the gong proclaimed the final race's conclusion.

Dao-sheng made his way through the crowd away from the river, to let his trousers dry in the sun and wind. He saw, from behind, the boy and two women making their way quickly toward the higher ground. His body was trembling, this body capable of saving a life and, though it had lost some of the vitality it once had, still capable of shuddering with desire.

Eighteen

WHAT DAO-SHENG HAD LEARNED BY CHANCE DURING THE festival of Duan-wu was confirmed the following month: Second Lord was now gravely ill. Why does a person fall sick at a particular moment? External causes are easy to find. The inner reasons are more difficult to discern, for of these even the patient himself is often unaware. That Second Lord was suffering from the inevitable consequences of his paralysis was undeniable. Yet someone of more serene disposition suffering the same affliction might have lived with it for far longer. The man who was accustomed to exercising power as he pleased, and who took joy from uncontested domination, was gnawed at from within by rage. This rage exacerbated his feelings of impotence and negated his ability to appreciate simple pleasures, such as those given him by Lady Fu-chun. He was not so stupid as to fail to realize that her feelings toward him were forced and false; nothing could change that. Yet how dependent he was upon her. However, had he been able to let go, had he stopped working so hard at controlling matters and expecting so much in return, life might have proceeded in tranquil fashion. A little pain here, a little suffering there, nothing fatal.

But all that didn't take into account a most unexpected event. Lady Ying's metamorphosis had taken him by complete surprise. He still didn't understand how this sad and disappointed woman, steeped in her religion, had suddenly become so desirable. The very fact that he himself was not the reason was intolerable. This woman whom he had cast aside was permitting herself to be happy in her little world, while he, the master of the house, spent more time each day awash in squalid depression.

Her incredible appeal was a constant provocation. It lit within him an evil fire that was slowly devouring him. Here was the truth: You can become miserable through jealousy for the happiness—even if imagined—of another. This is all the more true when the person in question belongs to you. Lady Ying was still his wife. Once, all Second Lord had had to do was lift a finger to summon or dismiss her. Some aberration had led to this humiliating change in situation, in which a combination of impotence, blunder, and embarrassment conspired to make his simply making love to his own wife impossible.

Ever since that disastrous meeting when Lady Ying had escaped his clutches, Second Lord had been stewing. He was plotting a second attempt. The more he thought about her, the more acute his desires became. It seemed to him now that for all eternity only she—her hair, her shoulders, her arms, her breasts, her thighs—might satisfy him, even though once she had inspired merely boredom, even disgust. Such is the power of the human imagination. So consuming was his hunger that Second Lord was sick from it.

Dao-sheng knew nothing about all this, of course, but one didn't need to be a soothsayer to know that this man was violent, handled his paralysis badly, and sooner or later would die. Could one predict how soon? The answer was no. Nor what consequences his disease would have.

In the meanwhile, Second Lord's rule over the house was absolute. The smallest thing enraged him. He demanded complete silence and forbade all activity he considered irritating or pointless. The children could not play in the garden, Lady Fu-chun and Jiao-ma could not visit with the neighbors or chat with peddlers, Lady Ying had to cease the folly of the midday food distribution, and so on. Even Lao- Sun, who was Second Lord's only servant after the departure of Zhu the Sixth, was affected. He had to attend to Second Lord without reprieve—running errands and with help from the guards transporting the doctor to come see him, often every night.

Thus Lan-ying was housebound. For someone as well bred as she, there was no question of permitting her feet to touch the road. She managed with Lao Sun's help to go to the temple two or three times during the sixth month. He knew of her need to pray and burn incense. With the complicity of one of the guards, he took advantage of his master's nap to carry her in the chair to town, then waited nervously until she was finished. The trip back to the house was as hurried as the trip out.

The haste with which Lan-ying appeared and then disappeared threw Dao-sheng into profound distress, though it only made what he felt when he saw her more intense. With her air of melancholy mixed with earnestness, she truly did evoke

Guan-yin. There was something different in her appearance, and Dao-sheng soon figured out it was her hair. She had drawn it up onto her head in a bun, held with a hair stick. This made her face even more attractive.

Far from being defeated, she feels the desire to speak—with her body. That was the thought that consoled Dao-sheng. He was struck again by how few men pay enough attention to what women do with their appearance. They are content merely to appreciate the final result, without distinguishing the emotionally charged elements that go into creating the ensemble, such as the elegant way the arm is raised to comb the hair or knot it with nimble, delicate fingers. In the changing light that marked this time of the year, Lan-ying's presence startled Dao-sheng. It seemed as if each time he saw her was the very first. During the previous two years he had not observed her with such intensity, as he had been sure that he would see her every day. Now, looking was communicating, making beauty emerge. Beauty was not only exterior; it was not a point fixed forever, so that whenever you liked you could use it as an altar upon which to set a statue. It was a fountain at once visible and invisible, rising instantly from the depths of those gathered in appreciation of it. It was contact, sometimes unexpected, always exceeding expectation, and only the attentive could make it stunning and marvelous and unique.

Beauty is fragile. The truth of this Dao-sheng knew painfully. Riding the crest of the moment, it could vanish with the slightest carelessness. Cruelty and brutality snuff it out. Can beauty exist without anyone to see it? What is it about love that brings it so close, that is so tightly tied to it? Like love, beauty is a form of connection.

Dao-sheng wondered again about Second Lord and his illness, and whether his ban on activity would continue until the very end. Were something to happen to Second Lord, it might make being with Lan-ying easier. Or it could have precisely the opposite effect—the proprieties of widowhood would make contact more difficult. How he wanted something solid to lean upon. Caught up in a passion that was very real but whose mystery seemed endless, he realized once again how we are given life by the faith we carry within, a faith born of intuition or of experience. We would be crushed without it. If love was "more enduring than Heaven-Earth," it was because he believed it and because Lan-ying believed it. That stranger from beyond the Ocean of the West also believed it as well.

Dao-sheng suddenly felt it unpardonable that he had not gone back to visit this man who spoke of love and eternity. He and Lan-ying had pledged eternity to each other. Would he live up to his part? Life was so short, so fraught. How was he to overcome separation from her body? How was he to survive its absence? What remained of the breath, the soul?

Dao-sheng rose and went to the inn at the Southern Gate. He learned that the two men from the West were no longer lodged there. Invited by the police prefect, they had moved into a house next to the *ya-men*. Hearing this, Dao-sheng hesitated. He didn't have the heart to go there. "Perhaps I will see them again," he told himself. "Fate will decide. That is how the world works."

The sixth month flew by; the torrid heat of the seventh month arrived. Days passed without any sight of Lan-ying. One evening, Dao-sheng was in the middle of gathering up his things when Xiao-fang appeared. She told him that her mistress was in good health but suffered from not being able to leave the house. As she spoke, Xiao-fang glanced quickly around her. When she thought no one was looking, she slipped him a slim package, which he put into his large pocket.

Back in his room, Dao-sheng waited until no noise was coming from the corridor before opening the package. Doors at the monastery were not locked; no one assumed he had a private life. Dao-sheng's hands shook. The paper envelope contained something square-shaped—a bag, barely larger than a hand, closed by tiny buttons. Inside was a folded embroidered cloth. On one side was a water scene stitched in pale green, with an aquatic plant here and there. In the foreground was a flower, an orchid; further off, near the other side, a white lotus. Between the two flowers, as if to cheer them up, swam a reddish fish. The ripples it made as it moved heedlessly through the water were artfully rendered.

After first admiring the skill with which each figure was embroidered, Dao-sheng gave the piece his serious attention. He was sure that it bespoke Lan-ying's heart. He wondered whether its message could be deciphered. During the Festival of the Moon, they had had so much to say to each other that they had said only a few things. Now, taking advantage of her imprisonment, Lan-ying had sewn her thoughts with the finest thread, stitch by stitch. She was asking him to read them. The images, so full of life and yet so simply done, seemed to combine boldness with modesty, the straightforward and the oblique. Here was a painting and a poem. The question was, What did it say?

Gathering up his thoughts, Dao-sheng remembered his friend and neighbor the scholar, the perennial examination taker. He had taught Dao-sheng how to read poetry, to find and to understand what lay between and beyond words. Dao-sheng wished he could show the scholar the embroidered cloth right away and listen to his interpretation of it. Knowing that he couldn't do that, he began to remember what his friend had instructed him about classical poems, whose relevance remained undiminished, and whose charm and wisdom the scholar brought to life. Dao-sheng heard in his mind the quavering voice of the man who regarded himself as such a failure. "To express longing for your native land, you could say, 'I would like to see my homeland once again.' That's brief and direct. But the poet writes:

> The cold plum branches outside the window—
> Did they flower when spring came?

"He remembers the past, imagines the present, and places his hope in the future. Plum branches blossom every spring, and one day he will see them again. Or he will find them blossoming somewhere else—and wherever plum trees blossom, there is his home.

"To express a thought about a friend living far away, you might say, 'I think about you every night.' That's to the point. But the poet writes:

> The pinecone falls on the empty mountainside.
> The man far away, too, must be lying awake.

"He's recalling when he was with his friend and they listened to sounds, knowing that when they were apart they would listen to the same sounds, like that made by a falling pinecone, or their hearts beating in unison."

Then there was the ancient verse the scholar loved best, the one about two lovers parting.

"The man moves off in a boat, the woman remains behind on the shore. The poem, a quatrain, ends like this:

> On the lake the voyager returns:
> A green mountain surrounded by a white cloud.

"At first glance, one might easily see the green mountain as the woman on the shore, and the white cloud as the man heading off. A better reading might be that the green mountain, the *yang,* is the man, who seems to cry from far off, 'I'm leaving but my thoughts stay with you,' and that the white cloud, the *yin,* would be the woman murmuring, 'I'm staying but my heart goes with you.' This last verse reminds us of an eternal truth: The cloud is formed among mountain deeps. It rises up into the sky, turns into rain, which, falling upon the mountain, makes it green again. The mountain forever holds the cloud, and the cloud forever holds the mountain. Here is constant motion, an unbreakable, ceaselessly renewing embrace that ordinary language can manage only to suggest."

The message of all this was, Never express your feelings directly. "Images say more." Dao-sheng wondered again what Lan-ying wanted to communicate in this embroidery.

"I know we cannot understand everything, so long as we are living this drama. For now, this is what I see. There is an orchid. There is a fish turning toward the orchid. Between the flower and the fish is the water, which unites them and keeps them apart. The lotus flower lies further off, as bright and as inaccessible as the moon. Does it represent your body or your soul? Is it calling to the fish and telling it to turn its head toward she who is closer to the other shore? 'To climb the other shore all you need to do is turn,' as the Buddhists say. We are on this bank. What lies on the other? Lan-ying, how I wish you could tell me in person. Yet I know that seeing each other is a gift refused us, and that even if we were together you would never tell me anything directly, because of modesty. Perhaps even you don't know what this means. You feel there are two flowers inside you, the orchid and the lotus. Between them is the fish, full of dreams and desires, yearning for some kind of clarity. Perhaps all he has to do is choose between them, or not choose at all. You chose to leave all this in suspension, so simple and yet as deep as the water."

The next day, Dao-sheng bought a ribbon that he sewed onto the little bag, then slipped it around his neck and carried it against his chest. Whenever he felt the need, he took the embroidery out and caressed the soft material, rubbing his fingers along the designs. He thought again of that handkerchief he had kept with him during his exile, then lost when he escaped. Touching that handkerchief had been like touching Lan-ying, rescuing him from loneliness and despair. He caressed this embroidery with the same intensity, yet with less urgency, less fierceness than thirty years before. Now it was with greater assurance and sweetness, with a more patient and attentive ear, with greater compassion. There was no longer any need to feel so caught up in some grand tragedy that it drains your body and your spirit. He was no longer the young man who had to embrace every flower, every bird, and every star. Once, going to a woman and having her was the simplest thing in the world. That was what he had thought. Love had become so enigmatic, an awareness that was equally painful and intoxicating.

Sitting on his bed on the evening of the third day of the Festival of the Double Seven, Dao-sheng watched as the two fated stars, the Herdsman and the Weaver, entered the Milky Way on their way to finding each other again. His emotions were not what they had been the year before. He had decided that he really was the fish, and that he could swim to his beloved. He thought of the joy he would feel at finding Lan-ying next month, during the Festival of the Moon.

Nineteen

IN HIS SOOTHSAYING PRACTICE, IN WHICH HE COMBINED elements of physiognomy, astrology, reading of hexagrams, as well as that kind of prescience born of long experience, Dao-sheng's predictions were very often extremely accurate. The same didn't hold true when applied to his own life. He lived now in the realm of passion, which engages instinct and desire on the one hand and morality and belief on the other. Add to that the mystery of woman. Without so much as a distant look or significant exchange, his ability to foresee clearly weakened. He had foreseen nothing of what had happened since he'd met Lan-ying again, nor could he even guess what was to come. He avoided thinking about it too much, for fear of ruining what Heaven had thus far given him. Doing nothing was the best thing. Lan-ying had given him her heart. What more was there to ask?

Meanwhile, Second Lord, displeased with the official doctors' treatment of his suffering, decided to consult one of those "charlatans," to see what he might be able to do. He meant, of course, Dao-sheng. Duly summoned, Dao-sheng wondered whether or not he should agree to see his old adversary. Yet he also knew deep down that he would not refuse. To come face-to-face with the man who had changed the course of his life was somehow unavoidable. Naturally he would not seek revenge; he and Second Lord lived on different levels now. Nonetheless, this man's request presented a challenge, and he would try to meet it with dignity. Accustomed to leading a double life, Dao-sheng had learned self-control; he also knew that within him was anger he would do well to be wary of.

Dao-sheng was led into a large room overlooking a garden. It smelled of opium and medicine. The man with the wrinkled forehead and contorted mouth was not immediately recognizable as the arrogant young man of long ago. The throbbing temples and eyes bulging with fever bespoke a lifetime of accumulated vice, corrupted by frustrated desires.

"I requested your presence, Master Soothsayer, because I know of your reputation in medicine. You cured my wife some time back. The doctors have given up on me, though they have done what they can. I cough up blood, I am racked by pains in my intestines, and I can barely relieve myself. What a miserable way to live!"

Dao-sheng said nothing in reply. He raised Second Lord's eyelids, studying the way the whites of the eyes were traversed by red lines. He asked Second Lord to cough, which the sick man did, dryly, and afterward extended his tongue for Dao-sheng to examine. The tongue was covered with a layer of green;

Dao-sheng recoiled at the man's breath. He was inches away from the man who thirty years before had been in a foaming rage against him. In this great, silent chamber, his old enemy was entirely at his mercy.

I will do nothing, Dao-sheng told himself. This man destroyed my life and that of Lan-ying, but she and I share a kind of happiness he could never imagine. There is no reason now for me to compare myself with this creature distorted by rancor. I wonder why I came here today. Curiosity, perhaps. Perhaps from a need to know whether this old tyrant feels even a shred of repentance.

He took Second Lord's pulse and very quickly diagnosed that the illness had become acute. With an appropriate though radical remedy, the inevitable might perhaps be delayed.

He was considering what medication to prescribe when the harsh voice came again. "I'm suffering! I'm in agony! I've never done anything that Heaven should treat me this way. How I *suffer!*"

The repetition of his complaint awoke the voice of fate, a fate that would not spare these two protagonists. The man who had determined to do nothing could not now stop himself from replying, "What you say is only partly true."

"Explain yourself."

"What you are suffering, good sir, is pain. Nothing is more real. But compared with what others have had to suffer unjustly, it is not so extreme. You might even consider yourself lucky."

"What do you mean? What injustices?"

"They are everywhere. You yourself have caused more than your share."

The words had come out before Dao-sheng could stop them.

"What do you mean by this?"

"I mean that, if you looked into your heart, you know you would find the wrongs you have committed in your life."

"How dare you speak so insolently?"

"I neither presume nor pretend to be insolent. Were you to look at it with a little humility and repentance, you would find your life has not been so miserable in comparison with others. It would be difficult to enumerate all the harms you have inflicted: Taxing the peasants, until they were forced to sell their children to survive. Violating women, then turning them into concubines or selling them off. Abusing alcohol and striking people whenever you pleased. Using your privilege to condemn innocent men to forced labor."

Dao-sheng had not intended to include this last point. He had gotten carried away.

"Condemning people to forced labor? I never did that!"

Being accused of something so unfounded bolstered Second Lord's sense of outrage. He couldn't take seriously someone who would make such wild accusations. He was about to take back the upper hand, to counterattack with self-righteous shrillness, when suddenly a memory came to him from out of the depths. Before his eyes appeared a cart, filled with prisoners bound together, taking them off to . . . forced labor. He stared hard at Dao-sheng, seeking out some distinctive feature, like an ancient scar on his left cheek.

"You! You are . . .?"

Dao-sheng ignored Second Lord.

"So long as the accounting of the heavenly numbers is unfinished, one continues to live. When these numbers reach their end, nothing more can humanly be done. You have been allowed your full share. No one has cheated you. What I said before is therefore the truth: Compared with the misery of others, you may consider yourself lucky."

Having finished what he wished to say, Dao-sheng rose unhurriedly, opened the door, and quietly departed from the Zhao estate.

"Criminal! Convict! You won't get far! I'll have you arrested! Wait and see!"

Incapable of feeling someone else's pain, Second Lord was possessed of startling imaginative resources when the matter concerned him. After the departure of the man he believed had disappeared forever, he quickly pieced together everything that had happened between Dao-sheng and Lady Ying. Images unfolded before his eyes like a scroll, to thunderous noise. His frail body began to tremble violently.

"Misery of all miseries! Disaster! I cannot bear the shame of this . . . creature staining the name of the Zhao family. The passing of eighteen generations won't wash this clean. I thought I had married a girl from a good family. I married a slut! Worse! The slut of a fake monk!

"You had probably already been soiled, that night in the great room with your pathetic family, the birthday party of your grandfather. Oh, yes. I remember how you looked at that reprobate musician. You were being coy with this phony, and this thief knew just how to take advantage of you.

"That's still true, isn't it? Thirty years later, and somehow he managed to find you again. Every time you went to the temple, you stopped before his filthy little stand, didn't you? You couldn't say much to each other, but you could exchange looks and smiles. Looks and smiles don't seem like a lot, but they can be thrilling, can't they? Oh, yes. A flower on the lips, the eyes all runny with emotion. You exchange speechless words: One sings and then the other responds, and then you start a silent little duet that just melts the heart away. *That's* the kind of happiness Second Lord will *never* know, isn't that so? I take women when I please, when the need arises, without formalities. With me they don't give these complicated, embroidered feelings, which now that I think about them are just so appetizing.

"Oh, but it didn't stop with a smile and a look, now did it? Oh, no no no. This phony Taoist came by every day for his free meal. When he held out his bowl to you, did you take advantage to give his hand a little caress? What am I saying? A little caress? I almost forgot that he took care of you when you were sick. How long was that? A month, maybe two. Each time he came, he put your hand in his. Ah, yes, hand to hand, palm to palm, what exquisite pleasure! Silent fingers, sweetly whispered words, the intoxication that spreads through the veins until it reaches the top of your skull and the soles of your feet, until you collapse in ecstasy. It's disgusting! You slut, you would be capable of this! Finding a happiness I didn't know. Me, with women, I take the shortest route. None of these fine, fine feelings.

"Since you two were capable of this kind of shamelessness, there's no way of knowing that you didn't take advantage of things to do more. You know, it's just possible! With Xiao-fang as their accomplice, this lowlife might have gotten into her bed! I have read my share of erotic books. I know these things can happen more easily than among dogs! The shame! I can't stand it! This will be the end of me. I see the two of them, naked, writhing in each other's arms, satisfying each other. The thought of it makes my chest explode!

"You will die and disappear. They will remain. After you're gone, no further need to be secretive about it. No need to hurry now! They can do it all day long, month after month, year after year! Endless tender caresses, endless cries of ecstasy! Nooooo! I'm suffocating!"

Twenty

"DID SECOND LORD CRY OUT? WHAT IS THE MATTER? HAS THE Taoist doctor gone?"

"Fu-chun! Fu-chun, come closer. Closer! Listen to me. Something horrible has happened, the most horrible thing you can imagine. You have to know. It's a matter of life or death!"

The words came spilling out of the stricken man, who was panting from rage.

"A matter of life or death?"

"I'm going mad. I never believed something like this would happen! That Taoist doctor, as you call him, do you know who he is? A bastard who dared to pick a fight with me thirty years ago. I had him arrested and sent to the *ya-men*. He was condemned to forced labor. He was worthless, so I forgot all about him. Now he has come back. Not just come back but come into my house, like a fox into the henhouse! When I think that he was just here, as close as you are now. That he touched me! I cannot stand it!"

"He didn't do anything?"

"Luckily, I realized who he was. Otherwise he would have poisoned me."

"Yes, well . . ."

"What do you mean 'Yes, well'? He's an outlaw! We have to arrest him and throw him in prison!"

"How?"

"Go quickly and see First Lord. He knows the prefect of police. One word will do it. . . ."

"Is that all? Fine. I'll go."

"Wait! Wait. There's something else. Something worse, something scandalous. The most disgraceful thing of all."

"Disgraceful?"

"So much so that I cannot tell you what it is. But I must."

"What is it?"

"Something's happened between this scum and Lady Ying."

"What?"

Fu-chun was exasperating Second Lord. Why was she so dense? Someone of greater refinement would have guessed right away. He would have to start at the beginning.

"He used to be a musician, a violin player with a theater troupe. It was the year that Old Lord Lu was celebrating his seventieth birthday. The troupe came to perform. Lady Ying was barely eighteen. From behind the screen, she and this vermin exchanged glances."

"That's difficult to believe. Lady Ying was from a good family."

"I had no proof, of course—that's why I didn't pursue it— but I'm telling you that during the whole performance that bastard kept leering at her, and that's the absolute truth.

That was the reason for the fight when he wounded me."

"Since there is no proof, it might be best to let it go."

"Now I have proof that he's an adulterer."

This announcement shook Lady Fu-chun, whose conscience was scarcely clear.

"This charlatan treated Lady Ying, do you remember?" continued Second Lord.

"We asked him to come."

"Asked! He came on behalf of the Great Monk, who is not exactly trustworthy."

"That doesn't mean—"

"You're so naïve! He was holding her hand and taking her pulse. Flame near a dry log! And this went on for two months. Can't you imagine what happened?"

Lady Fu-chun blushed deeply. Second Lord was too caught up in his rage to notice.

"This is hard to believe."

"Stop being so naïve. It's exasperating!"

"If there were proof . . ."

"I may be paralyzed, but I am not blind. I've learned to observe. And because of that I see everything"—Lady Fu-chun's nerves jumped again—"and I see to the bottom of things. Do you know what I saw?"

"What did you see?" she replied, tensely.

"I saw that after she had recovered Lady Ying changed."

"It is true."

"She became young. She became beautiful."

"That is so."

"Sad as she was, she didn't grow uglier as she aged. Now

she's fresh and pretty. Doesn't that strike you as strange? Attractive enough that it makes a man want to . . .'"

"What is Second Lord trying to say?"

"It means what it means. We're off the subject. I was not fooled by any of this. For a while I had myself taken into town to watch Lady Ying on her little excursions."

"So that was why—"

"Don't interrupt me. I had the chair set down not far from the temple. From behind the curtain, I could see everything. And I saw everything. This whole game of looks and whispers."

"Why didn't Second Lord tell me of this then?"

"At the time I didn't know who this charlatan really was. He was pretending to be a soothsayer. When Lady Ying greeted him as she passed, it seemed completely normal. I see things more clearly. Coming out of the temple, she always left by the same route, never deviating even once. So they made eyes at each other and said sweet things. Now I understand why Lady Ying kept giving away food to those wretches. Charity? I think not. She had her own pleasure in mind. I still call her Lady Ying, but she's a slut. Used goods. Even if we sold her to a brothel, we wouldn't get much for her. This brings shame on the Zhao family! Our ancestors are turning in their graves. She must be punished. Otherwise I will not die in peace."

"What does Second Lord wish us to do?"

"She must pay with her life."

"With her life?"

"I don't have much longer to live. The end could come at any time. If she is not punished, you can expect much worse, believe me. With someone like him, who's been around, someone capable of anything, she . . . ."

"What does Second Lord have in mind?"

What Second Lord had in mind made no sense; the simple truth was he had begun to came apart. This was what Lady Fuchun thought, though she was careful to keep it to herself.

"Put arsenic in her tea. I have some here in a box. Her sin is too great. She must die."

"I cannot do that."

"You must do it!"

"I cannot. Even if you put a rope around my neck!"

Second Lord understood that insisting was pointless.

"We will speak no more of that. Go now and warn First Lord. This fake Taoist is an escaped convict. To allow him to remain at large and dupe people poses a public danger. It is imperative he be exposed. Otherwise I will not be able to die in peace. Go!"

Exhausted by the effort of his tirade, Second Lord collapsed on his pillows.

Did he fear dying? It was a question Second Lord no longer had the strength to reflect upon. Since he had been racked by terrible pains for months, some part of him longed for release. If he looked back over his life, he could see certain things that argued in favor of peace: Those glorious years of debauchery were followed by a state of dependency in which setbacks were accepted, rages swallowed, impotence resented, desires forever frustrated. Worse than death was the obsession that now overshadowed this last phase of his life—couples giving each other pleasure when he was no longer there.

"Jiao-ma!" he called out. "Summon Lady Ying. I wish to speak to her."

The time between Jiao-ma's departure and Lady Ying's arrival was short, but to Second Lord it seemed an eternity. It was long enough, at any rate, for one fate to be decided.

There was a knock at the door. Then came a voice. A woman's form moved to the middle of the room. "Second Lord called for me? I am here. How is Second Lord's health?"

After a lengthy coughing fit, he cleared his throat. "Not strong. 'A candle's flame in the open air; a breath of wind can snuff it out.'"

"Second Lord must not give in to despair. He must take care of himself and find hope."

"Come closer. I must speak with you."

Lady Ying was on her guard, fearing some strange new caprice from this man. His extreme feebleness, however, was reassuring.

"Don't be afraid," Second Lord continued. "Come closer to me. I can't speak any louder, and I have something important to tell you. These will be the last words you will hear from me."

Moved by his sincere tone, Lan-ying approached Second Lord.

When she was next to him, he glared at her. "I'm going. I want to take you with me."

No sooner had he spoken these words than Second Lord's trembling hands suddenly stiffened and his heart was steeled with resolve. He quickly threw a cloth belt he had been holding around Lady Ying's neck and jerked it tight with all his

François Cheng

strength. The aged tyrant found his old might. He further tightened his grip, managing to spit out, "You and your filthy monk!"

He sensed she was fighting back but weakening. Then with a dry "ah," she collapsed on the floor and moved no more.

Second Lord threw himself back on the bed. His body went into convulsions. Then death planted a dagger in his heart.

Lady Fu-chun stayed for a while with First Lord, with whom she discussed at length how to accede to Second Lord's wishes. Without actual proof, punishing Lady Ying was out of the question. However, they decided that some kind of action needed to be taken against Dao-sheng. He had been banished and yet had returned. First Lord said he would go to see the prefect, though he also made it clear that the days when the Zhao family could dictate the law were over.

The concubine dragged her feet on the way back. She was not keen to face her master again. The business between Lady Ying and Dao-sheng shocked her. It also made her think. She had her own story, and were it ever to come to light, she would deserve an ignominious death. The thought made her shudder.

When she entered Second Lord's room, her fear was replaced by stunned surprise. He was immobile on his bed, at the foot of which lay Lady Ying. When she saw the belt, Lady Fu-chun understood immediately.

"And so it was fatal. It could not have been otherwise."

She picked up the belt, closed the mouth and eyes of Second Lord, and then closed those of his wife. She straightened the collar of the dead woman's dress. Then she called Jiao-ma and asked her to help lift Lady Ying's body onto the bed and place it next to Second Lord's. Lady Fu-chun offered no explanations, as if it were obvious that the legitimate wife of Second Lord had died of shock upon seeing the body of her husband.

This was also what she told Xiao-fang, who replied that for the sake of decency her mistress's body needed to be returned to her own chambers. The three women carried Lady Ying to her bed.

Feeling as though the sky had fallen down around her, Xiao-fang kept vigil over the body.

Twenty-one

"DEATH BRINGS WITH IT DEATH, LIFE BRINGS LIFE." SO THE ancient philosophers used to say with confounding simplicity. What the dead bequeath to the living—if these dead had ever once been truly alive—is grief but also a powerful sense of the duty of living, of finishing that from which the dead have been separated, and that which remains behind. Thus the living put the dead on the Way of Life; thus they keep us from giving in to death.

Such, however, were not Xiao-fang's thoughts at that moment. From deep inside the abyss of her grief came a flash of light. "Lady Ying's life cannot end like this!" she cried. "Her numbers are not finished!"

These defiant words were her way of putting her mistress back on the Way of Life. Abandoning the dictates of discretion established by Lady Fu-chun, she ran out to find Lao Sun. She told him to go in search of Dao-sheng.

Dao-sheng was neither at his stand near the temple nor at the monastery. Not knowing where to turn, Lao Sun went to the teahouse. The serving girls suggested he go to the butcher's, but Dao-sheng wasn't there either. Finally, having asked everyone he knew, Lao Sun found him at the house of the scholar. He took Dao-sheng outside and told him in a rush the terrible news, how Lady Ying had been found dead in the room of Second Lord, who was also dead, and how she was now lying in her own room. No wound was visible.

Dao-sheng immediately guessed everything.

"There isn't a moment to lose," he said simply and broke into a run toward the Zhao estate.

Keeping pace behind him, Lao Sun wondered what Dao-sheng planned to do. What could anyone do?

As for Dao-sheng, he blamed himself. His remorse was so great that nothing, not even taking his own life, was sufficient punishment. He had sought refuge at the scholar's because he had known perfectly well that Second Lord would not let things go. But he would never have imagined their altercation would have had such consequences.

Led by Lao Sun, he entered Lan-ying's room. Xiao-fang was sitting next to the bed, sobbing softly. There was no time for explanations. Dao-sheng asked if she would leave the room with Lao Sun, making sure the door was closed behind them and seeing to it that no one came in. He walked toward the bed and drew open the curtain. Lan-ying lay before his eyes, wearing her light blue dress; her hands were folded across her chest. Her face was firm and serene, as if made of ivory or jade.

Dao-sheng started to tremble but regained control. He lifted Lan-ying's arm and placed it alongside her body, noting that it was not yet stiff. He stood up, looking again at her. He was gathering his powers of concentration, preparing for what he knew would be the greatest test of his life. If he failed, he would not survive. His forehead tensed; his eyes shone with a singular light.

"Lan-ying, I am here. You will not die!" he cried in a muffled voice.

He got down on his knees, undid her belt, opened her dress, and began to massage her body, starting with the soles of her feet and her ankles. Following the internal meridians, he moved up to the neck, then concentrated his energies there, upon the nape of the neck and the top of the spinal cord. After that, he massaged the chest, moving back and forth between the heart and the lungs. Once this series of motions was finished, he started working in the opposite direction, beginning with the neck and moving down to the feet. He returned to the chest and moved back and forth between the heart and the lungs. He started over again: feet to neck, neck to feet. Then a third time.

Tense though he was, Dao-sheng performed this procedure with great patience, not knowing how long it would take and not caring. He was using a technique based upon the hand's magnetic force that had been taught to him by the Great Monk. It involved looking for the formula that would help him join in with the Great Rhythm, to revive the circulation and breath, both within himself and the body that he was trying to bring back into the realm of the living. Fighting an enormous shadow on his own made him both noble and pathetic. Apart from his skill, he was equipped with only his humility and his sincerity, and did not know if they would be enough for him to reach the *shen*. It was as if he were throwing a rope across a vast gulf of space in the hope of catching a wild goose on the wing.

Sensing the moment was ripe, he halted his efforts and began to breathe deeply, all the way down to the *dan-tian,* the regions of mercury. Then he went back to work, with a heavy whistle punctuating every breath—a technique practiced by the Taoists for centuries. The moment of truth was at hand.

At that instant came a faint sign of life returning. Only Dao-sheng could perceive it. Had the Lord of the Heavens existed, He would have perceived it as well. At the end of the branch of a frozen tree, a bud was forming, or perhaps only the idea of a bud: a movement of the bloodless lips that was so nearly imperceptible that only the third eye could sense it. He delicately parted Lan-ying's lips, placed his mouth to them, pressing only very gently, and began to breathe, blowing air deep into her throat as rhythmically as he had massaged her. It was an act he had performed before in his life—on victims of drowning or heart attacks, on children accidentally strangled or old people choking on their food. This time, however, his intervention was coming late, and the person he was attempting to save was more precious than his own life. If necessary, he would expend the last ounce of breath he had.

He was nearing the point of exhaustion. Still he wouldn't stop. He did not wish to survive this woman.

There came a trembling of the lips. He felt it. Was the wild goose veering toward him? Then came more trembling. The bud was forming. The underground spring was rising to the surface. Lan-ying opened her eyes and saw Dao-sheng. A pale smile formed. Just as quickly, her eyes closed and her face shut down.

Dao-sheng, desperate, leaned in close. His alarm was short-lived. The breath of life, faint though it was, continued to create a faint wake. More perceptible was the movement of the chest, now beating with an internal rhythm.

Dao-sheng closed the light blue dress. He could do no more. He collapsed at the foot of the bed. His body shuddered with sobs.

He rose to his feet and looked at Lan-ying's body. Her respiration was maintaining its own equilibrium, independent of him. A silence, like some solemn presence come from far away, floated over them. He remembered what the Great Monk had said about the night he brought Lan-ying home from the mountains. "Between Heaven and Earth, a human being has been brought back to life." That was it exactly, except this time Lan-ying had come back from life's other side. Dao-sheng was suddenly aware of the sacred light flooding into the room. Soon he would leave, for the last time probably, this place in which something extraordinary had taken place. Where would fate now take him? Thoughts raced in his mind, and he gave them free rein. He wanted this moment to stretch out indefinitely.

"Being on this side of life is no ordinary thing," he said to himself. "Here is where the day is. Here is where the world is. In this room, there is she, and I, and what has happened between us. There is the furniture and the screen. The incense bowl filled with ashes, the table on which lies the unfinished embroidery, the perfume of the flowers that comes in waves from outside. Birds chatter and beat their wings. Yes, here is where the day is, where the world is. Everything is ordinary and seemingly indifferent. Yet everything happens, miraculously. He who survives will not forget. Whoever has lived will not be forgotten. That must be what eternity means. Lan-ying is back. Everything is possible once again. Can we do what we would like? After the miracle, how can we return to the ordinary?"

While saying this, Dao-sheng tenderly caressed the hands and face of the sleeping woman. Then he shook himself from his dreamlike state, walked to the door, opened it, and asked Xiao-fang and Lao Sun to enter, indicating with a gesture that they should make no noise. That was when they knew their mistress was saved. Incredulity mixed with fear. They went into the middle of the room. When they saw Lady Ying was breathing, they fell to their knees. Xiao-fang mumbled a prayer: *A-mi tuo-fo, a-mi tuo-fo*—Merciful Buddha, Merciful Buddha. Still on his knees, Lao Sun wheeled toward Dao-sheng and began bobbing up and down, his forehead striking the floorboard, as one might do before a living god.

Twenty-two

LAN-YING REMAINED IN BED, CLOISTERED IN HER ROOM, FOR quite some time. The funeral ceremonies for Second Lord lasted several days, after which the household entered a period of mourning. First Lord decided against reporting Dao-sheng to the *ya-men*. He knew what sort of trouble would ensue. Moreover, the itinerant doctor had saved Lady Ying's life, sparing the family from scandal. How lucky they had all been. No file documenting his having been sentenced to forced labor existed. Knowing his brother, however, First Lord did not doubt that a false accusation was involved. That said, this individual would never again be allowed to cross the threshold of the Zhao estate.

Lan-ying and Dao-sheng could communicate only by using Xiao-fang as an intermediary, and only after some time had passed. Mourning and the fear of being seen required absolute discretion. The first time, Xiao-fang came to ask for some medications to ease the pain her mistress continued to feel. She was not able to assure Dao-sheng that all was well; her mistress was still in a fragile state of health. A full month passed before

Xiao-fang could report that she was at last showing signs of improvement. She transmitted her mistress's thoughts, but in the most restrained terms.

Toward the end of the ninth month, Xiao-fang climbed the temple steps and remained inside for quite some time. When she came out, she informed Dao-sheng that Lady Ying had asked the Great Monk to intervene on her behalf, and that of her servant, with a convent in the Guan-yin Valley where they hoped to gain admission. Dao-sheng felt relief. This offered a temporary solution, and he could come up with no other. Beyond question it was wise for Lan-ying to leave the Zhao household. What would she do after her stay at the convent— if anything at all? That he couldn't forsee. He nervously awaited Xiao-fang's next visit. By then the Great Monk had arranged matters with the convent. So great was the holy man's joy that he expressed it during the collective prayers, proclaiming his gratitude to Buddha.

One day Xiao-fang arrived unexpectedly at Dao-sheng's stand. "Lady Ying wishes me to tell you that soon she will go and live in the convent. For how long, she does not know. Everything depends upon what she must do after that. That, too, she doesn't know. You must not push her to decide. One day she will give you a sign. She wonders if you cannot go back up the mountain and wait for her there. If you go, take Gan-er."

Dao-sheng's only response was to nod his head.

The Zhao family—and Lady Fu-chun in particular—regarded Lady Ying's departure for the convent as a blessing. They could see no reason why Gan-er should not become a bonze at the temple. For the moment that seemed to be what he wanted. Later he could do as he wished. He would be one less thing for the family to worry about.

For Dao-sheng and Lan-ying, everything took on new meaning, though her departure was a reenactment of what had happened so often these last few years. Carried in a chair by Lao Sun and one of the guards, Lan-ying and Xiao-fang went to the temple, followed by Gan-er. They lit incense sticks and expressed their gratitude to the Great Monk for his intercession. When they came out, Lan-ying headed for Dao-sheng's stand for what was doubtless the last time.

They were alone for a moment. Dao-sheng absorbed her presence, which was contained and unrestrained, real and distant, as tremulous as a whisper of autumn wind and so pale as to make you weep. Talking in a public place remained risky. Still, no one could deny the propriety of a patient saying farewell to her doctor, and for the first time Lan-ying was not held back by scruples.

"I am going to live for a while in the convent in the Guan-yin Valley. During this time I will see no one."

"And soon I will return to the mountain, where I will wait."

"Yes, wait. During the Festival of the Moon we swore we would be together, in this life and in the next. We will see each other again, Dao-sheng. I don't know when. We must be patient. For now we must do nothing. Heaven will reveal things in its own time."

His heart tightened.

"Yes," he murmured.

"We must be patient. When the time comes, I will send you a signal.

"Lan-ying, you must take very good care of yourself."

For a moment she did not respond. Mastering her emotions, she said, "Dao-sheng, I'm going now. Rising sun, setting sun, hidden moon, full moon, we will never forget each other for even a moment. Let us now always be together."

"We will never forget each other. We will now always be together, Lan-ying."

He wanted to add something more but found he couldn't speak. Through the mist covering his eyes, he saw her walk away, her back slightly hunched. She needed to lean on Xiao-fang to reach the chair. Before getting in, she turned, looked back, and then disappeared with Xiao-fang behind the curtain. The porters moved off briskly, and the chair soon disappeared in the crowd.

Sitting at his stand, Dao-sheng felt regret such as he had never known, and he had known much regret in his life—as an orphan, a traveling musician, a man condemned to forced labor, a fugitive. Yet no matter how hard things became, his invincible vitality had always seen him through. What was crushing him now did not come from outside. His heart, his very flesh, was being ground down by a nameless power. The heightened sense of reality in which he had lived for the last three months seemed suddenly to vanish like a chimera, like passing clouds. The happiness he had felt at the prospect of seeing Lan-ying every day was gone. Between Heaven and Earth hung emptiness. She had said that they would see each other again. When? In this life or another? Two lines of tears moved slowly down the length of his wrinkled cheeks. He didn't wipe them away. Indifferent to the looks of surprise on the faces of people who passed by, he was grateful no one thought of asking him for a prediction.

More patience. More waiting. Dao-sheng wondered whether he had even the strength to get up. Perhaps, he thought, it would help if he talked to someone. No one came to mind. The Great Monk? The monks at the monastery? The scholar? The butcher? How could he make anyone understand what had happened? They might react like Second Lord and see him as a rogue who had corrupted the virtue of a married woman. They might not understand that in this world there is a mysterious knot common law cannot undo.

He needed to find someone outside it all and yet able to understand. The religious stranger.

Dao-sheng said to himself, "He told me things that I couldn't quite understand, that I couldn't quite believe. Some of the things he said made sense. They touched me."

The thought of seeing this man again gave Dao-sheng the strength to gather himself. He took the road that led to the *ya-men*. It was a cursed place for him, but perhaps now that would change.

Many people were waiting in the foyer. Word had gotten around that the holy strangers would very soon be leaving for the capital; no one wanted to miss the opportunity of seeing them and speaking with them. Dao-sheng took a place among the crowd. Being with others distracted him from his loneliness, though he wondered as he looked at them what had brought them here. Some wearing scholars' robes were talking in what seemed a very refined language. These were disciples of Confucius, the great teacher who had exhorted men to engage in an endless process of self-improvement and perfectionism. He knew why they had come. They wanted to know more about the son of the Lord of the Sky, whom the stranger had said was a perfect man. Some came to express their skepticism, others to learn more, and still others either to mock or to act indignant. This was normal. People find what they seek; everyone listens to the one singing. But what of these nonscholars, these ordinary people sitting near him? Why were they here? He overheard fragments of their conversations.

". . . there were magic objects . . ."

". . . and to touch their hair and beard."

". . . skin color can't be natural, so I . . ."

". . . that bad times are coming and they speak of a savior."

The group of scholars was graciously invited into the room by one of the holy men. Dao-sheng knew it was his former patient who was greeting them. He not only spoke the language well but eloquently.

After a long while, the religious stranger himself, tall and straight in his scholar's robes, came back out, accompanying the visitors. Dao-sheng realized that this was the first time he had seen him upright. Near the door, after a final farewell gesture, he turned and glanced at the entry hall. His eyes met those of his former doctor. A smile spread across his face. "When a friend comes from afar . . ." he said, pronouncing in a hearty voice the beginning of a line from Confucius, and approaching Dao-sheng.

Realizing that these two men knew each other, the others willingly let Dao-sheng go ahead of them.

"I am so happy to see you again! I cannot thank you enough for curing me of the fever."

"I have not forgotten you either. Some of your words have remained with me."

"Is that true?"

"You spoke of love. You said that he who loves truly can say to his beloved, 'You will not die.'"

"I remember saying that."

"Well, I have spoken those words once. And I brought back to life someone who had been taken for dead."

"Is this true? This shows the glory of the Lord."

"Excuse me?"

"What happened was due to the glory of the Lord. Everything that is great and marvelous comes from Him."

"I . . . I had thought my success was due to connecting to the primordial Breath of Life."

After the briefest hesitation, the stranger replied. "There isn't necessarily any difference between them. But that would require lengthy discussion. I very much hope that we will be given an occasion to return to it. I am about to leave for the capital. You and I must part in a moment."

"Part! That is what is painful. I am parted from the person I love. It is agony."

"Those who truly love are always together. They are even more deeply bonded, whatever the distance or the time separating them."

"That sounds so beautiful, but are you sure of what you say? Have you loved someone?"

"Like everyone else, I have loved someone. My parents, my brothers, and my sisters . . ."

"I'm not talking about family. I'm talking about a woman, loving a woman to distraction."

"I never loved one woman in particular. I love humanity in general."

"Can you love humanity in general without having loved one with particular passion?"

"You speak of passion. I was just going to say that I love someone with passion, to distraction, as you put it."

"Who?"

"The Son of God."

"I had forgotten him. He is no longer here. And you never knew him personally."

"I know Him as if He were closer than I am to myself. Having known Him, I will never forget Him. He is no longer there and yet He is there, more than ever. He loves us. And if we love Him, we are always together, as I said before."

"I must ask again. Are you truly and absolutely convinced of what you say?"

"Why else would I have left my native land and those I love, to come and live here, and probably die here as well? Those who truly love each other are not limited either by distance or by time. Their souls are bound up together, and that is a tighter and more unbreakable union than that of the body."

"Not limited by time. Still, there will be an end, will there not?"

"There will be no end. Together in this life, together after death."

"You believe that?"

"I do. 'You will not die.' That you remember. I do not think you have forgotten the Chinese expression 'more enduring than Heaven and Earth' that we talked about last time?"

"I have not forgotten. What I need to know now is whether it is beyond doubt."

"The guarantee offered by the Lord of the Heavens is love, and He is eternal life."

"If he is eternal life, why then did he create death?"

"You have asked this question. Answering it would take a long time. When people come from so far away, much time is required to understand each other. One day we will. For now, I will simply say that it is because we are all sinners."

"We are all sinners and we must die. It is so strange."

Dao-sheng remained silent for a moment. Then he asked, "Therefore, is loving a sin?"

"How can loving be a sin? It is the Divine itself. But there are ways of loving that are sins."

"Which ones?"

"Well, for example, when you love a married woman."

"Ah. Even when no love exists between a husband and wife, when their marriage had been arranged?"

The man who had a reply to everything did not respond right away. He thought for a moment, and then, almost as if he were talking to himself, he said, "It is true that one of our saints has said, 'Love and do what you will.'"

The two men entered gently into silence. Many things between them remained unexplained or incommunicable. Yet when they looked at each other, they knew that a deep affection had formed within the space of the middle void.

"Thank you," said Dao-Sheng as he prepared to leave. "It was my great fortune to meet someone like you. You have come from across the Ocean of the West. I am a man without a home. I see love as you see love, a love perhaps more restrained but surely no less intense."

"Thank you for everything, Dao-sheng. You are a man of

great heart. I believe that you have understood a great deal. In your way you have already found what you seek. Your questions force me to think. It was my great fortune to have met you. It has been worth coming to the Middle Kingdom for this. Will our paths cross again? It matters little. We are already friends, and now we will never forget each other."

"In this life as well as after death?"

"We leave together for eternity."

The two men smiled conspiratorially. The stranger took his visitor in his arms and embraced him, aware that the Chinese found this sort of gesture shocking; they generally greeted or parted without touching hands other than their own.

Twenty-three

AUTUMN PASSED, WINTER CAME AND WENT, AND THEN IT WAS again the middle of spring. Six months had gone by since Lan-ying had left for the convent. Dao-sheng still lived in the town. His self-pity had not left him, and he still felt divided. On the one hand, staying made Lan-ying's absence that much more painful. On the other hand, everything and everyone reminded him of her: the poor seeking food, who now gathered in other parts of the town, with their usual complaints and preoccupations; the believers who mounted and descended the temple steps; the chair porters, each ruddier than the one before, sitting in the teahouses; the light from the setting sun that flooded the square, as if announcing an apparition.

Dao-sheng had not thought himself capable of climbing the mountain during the cold months. Moreover, in town, he felt closer to Lan-ying. He half-expected to see her. He also couldn't simply abandon his patients and clients, or his friends, particularly the butcher and the scholar.

The most unexpected thing was the helping hand extended to him—how could he have predicted such a thing?—by Lao Sun. This faithful servant had succeeded in buying back Shun-zi, perhaps because of his very fidelity. Lao Sun had not saved enough money to do it and couldn't have, even if he had hoarded every copper coin for fifteen years. Lan-ying had helped him. Having learned of the situation before leaving the Zhao household, she had given him her most precious jewels. Thus was the circle of fate enclosed in a bracelet. Lan-ying's magnificent gesture to Lao Sun had redounded to Dao-sheng. The taciturn former peasant felt profound gratitude to the traveling doctor, the savior of Lady Ying, and regularly invited him to the lodging that he and his new wife had rented on the outskirts of town.

Shun-zi, who had said that three lifetimes of service to whomever liberated her from the brothel would not be enough, was as good as her word. From nothing she seemed to create a home where one could find all the simple pleasures. Touched by Lao Sun's goodness and by the miracle of her own change in destiny, she found a way of mending her wounds. The youthful freshness of the girl she had once been had remained, miraculously, intact. She also proved a superb cook. She could put some vegetables, soy paste, a few herbs, and some lard into a pot and produce the most succulent meals. When he tasted them, Dao-sheng was so overwhelmed that he almost could not eat. The vegetables Lan-ying had served the poor had given off the same aroma. Remembering the Buddhist law about cause and effect, he was almost convinced that Lan-ying had helped Lao Sun buy back Shun-zi for this reason as well—to help him, Dao-sheng, ease the abruptness of her disappearance.

It was a period of transition. Lao Sun worked for a while as a porter near the main gates of the city. Before long he was hired by a large family in another city; honest and experienced servants were not easy to find during these troubled times. He and Shun-zi had to abandon the man they had adopted with such full hearts, and they did so with great unhappiness.

Dao-sheng was alone again. Except for the Great Monk and Gan-er, he had no contact with people who were connected to Lan-ying. The time to leave had come. Gan-er, though now well-settled into the life of the temple, was ready to follow him. This growing young man considered Lady Ying his mother and Dao-sheng his father. The Great Monk proved again a man of surprisingly broad understanding. He knew that from Dao-sheng Gan-er would learn medicine and soothsaying. As for what happened later, well, fate would decide.

In the third month, the Festival of *Qing-ming*—when sacrifices are made to the dead—came and went. Master and disciple climbed up the mountain. The seven Taoist monks were still alive. One of them had grown too old to do much of anything. Two others suffered from severe rheumatism and had difficulty taking part in communal tasks. Fewer worshippers came now, and the monastery was in a fearful state of decay. Dao-sheng's returning, and bringing with him a young recruit, was a godsend. The two got to work almost right away, fixing holes and breaks in the outer walls and leaks in the roof. One urgent task during this second half of spring was to plant the kitchen garden. It was lucky that Gan-er possessed such boundless energy, for Dao-sheng felt his strength diminishing.

Despite being perhaps slightly more pale, Dao-sheng appeared unchanged to the monks. No one guessed that his heart was breaking. Yet he would have been incapable of explaining this to others. Things that once haunted him now seemed irrelevant. His life centered on only one thing: Waiting.

He had known the pangs of waiting when Lan-ying had been ill, and when she had been forbidden to leave the house. One counted, drop by drop, the time flowing by, the days and the nights, unable to think of anything else. Yet the proximity of the beloved and the hope of seeing her again were sustaining.

This time, the displacement, the distance, and the uncertainty conspired to send Dao-sheng into an altered state of awareness. Memories overpowered the present. The smallest details of his shared life with Lan-ying pressed themselves upon him with astounding clarity. Past and present mingled. He lived in two places at once: Here and there. He participated mechanically in daily rituals and tasks. "Rising sun, setting sun, hidden moon, full moon, we will never forget each other"—the phrase echoed in his ears, like a song learned in childhood.

In the morning, on his way back from the well, he put the buckets of water he was carrying on grass wet with dew. Through the mist he gazed at the distant valley, across which wound countless paths. At the end of one was the outline of Lan-ying, which grew clearer the nearer she came. There she was in the doorway, at the back of the garden, in her light blue dress, smiling. In twilight, after the sun had disappeared below the summit, warm light still bathed the uppermost rock faces. He usually remained sitting quietly by himself after prayers were finished. He could see Lan-ying approaching, giving him a sign, and looking at him, then, wordlessly, moving away.

Night was a passage he learned to navigate. Candle in hand, he entered his room. The flickering light projected his shadow against the wall, and this sight distracted him. He had maintained the habit of sleeping sitting up and fully clothed. Leaning against his pillows, he drew the blanket up to his chest or shoulders, trying not to mind when sleep didn't come. He looked at the back of his hand on the blanket, lit by the light from the moon or the stars, a hand with rugged skin, roughened and misshapen. Invariably another hand, one dazzlingly white by contrast, settled gently on his, covering and warming it. Sometimes it was the other way around. His hand reached for the outstretched palm of the other, which matched its pressure, whether timid or fervent. And still other images came to him, these incandescent, passing through his body. He neither fought them nor acted upon them.

Night sometimes brought unexpected things. The empty mountainside echoed with the slightest sounds, which reached his ears with overwhelming clarity. The wind amplified the rustle of falling leaves; the owls screeched their irremediable solitude. When a storm approached, the thunder made the shutters shake and so, too, the body of the wakeful listener. After a long silence, in which the hollow universe held its breath, the rains came in torrents, bringing with them the odor of roots and mosses from the mountain places through which they had rushed, like unleashed beasts and unchained hearts endlessly spewing out their heartbreak. Even when the rains diminished, their power was prolonged in the numberless waterfalls that from rock to rock echoed their unappeasable song. As the ancient poet had written, Dao-sheng knew that in the valley another wakeful spirit was listening.

When the hot weather came, pilgrims started to arrive in growing numbers. At the beginning Dao-sheng felt a pang whenever he saw someone approaching on the path. A messenger from the convent? That was of course his first thought, and he was always disappointed. To avoid this, he tried to focus his attention upon the pilgrims, all the more since among them were sick people to whom, with Gan-er's assistance, he started offering consultations. He wondered whether he had ever been interested in people for their own sakes—to anything like the degree Lan-ying had been. When he summoned from within him all his empathy, he saw what good results it instantly produced. The desire to reach out to others brought him closer to Lan-ying; it also distracted him. He was gripped by a revelation: That at the heart of even the most frightening of human predicaments, about which so many sought to acquire wisdom and perspective, there were treasures to explore. That was why the holy stranger had come from so far.

"He acted in the name of his lord in Heaven. I act in the name of what I was given. Each seeks his own kind of completion, following the lines of his own destiny."

Dao-sheng looked at the elderly women who arrived at the monastery out of breath but full of humble dignity. Their wrinkled and pocked faces carried the accumulation of countless pains and sorrows. They had simple but graceful ways, practiced over the course of long lifetimes. Lighting sticks of incense, they joined their hands in prayer and thanked in a singsong voice their *Tai-shang-lao-jun,* their supreme master. Afterward, feeling almost lighthearted, they found a corner of the courtyard in which to chat, as well as to rest up before going back down the mountain.

One of them broke away from the others and approached Dao-sheng. "Venerable one, you live so near to Heaven, plead on our behalf with the celestial Master!"

Dao-sheng responded with a smile. Deep in her eyes he could see the young girl with unfulfilled dreams; he recognized as well the figure of the mother, though of his own he had no image.

Festival of the Moon. Midnight. The full moon transformed the earth into luminous pearl. Human passion, also crystallized, illuminated the night with a clarity that was as precious as it was fragile. Looking from afar at the same heavenly body, parted lovers have only to remember what they said to each other through the beating of their hearts in unison.

Alone in his room, Dao-sheng touched the bottom of his despair. Everything he had done to maintain a precarious peace with existence was crumbling. He wanted to cry, then go down the mountain and walk until he was with her.

He left the room and stood in the center of the courtyard, not knowing what to do. Wisteria vines climbing the wall hurled their perfume at him; crickets chirred ceaselessly their parched cries. Nature followed its course, indifferent.

Under the pretext of seeking tea, he went to wake Gan-er.

The young man rubbed his sleepy eyes. He saw the gaunt figure of Dao-sheng in the moonlight. As if by divine instinct, he was moved to ask, "We have been far from Lady Ying for months now. When is she going to give us a sign so that we can go see her?"

"Yes, when is she going to give us a sign? Without it we must not go to her. She said so."

Dao-sheng didn't return to his room until the fourth watch. He was tired yet didn't feel like lying down. He leaned over the bed, thinking he could see Lan-ying through the curtain, and began his plea:

"The better part of a year has passed. This is hard, Lan-ying—having no news of you. You said that we would see each other one day, and that we needed to be patient. I understand that. I am thinking only of myself, still in a hurry for satisfaction—forgetting everything you have endured, and from what torments you need to recover. But how are we to be together? We must consider that. I do not know if I can think as you do. A woman's thought is more complex, more subtle, yet it touches upon what is true in life. It is more at peace with the pace of the world. Can I match it?"

His words calmed him. They opened up a space in which true dialogue could gain a foothold.

"Yes, enter into a woman's thoughts," he heard himself say. "Enter into Lan-ying's thoughts. That is what you must do from now on, for it is what you can do."

Several nights later, he felt the need to speak again.

"Well-bred woman that you are, possessed of such great sweetness, from infancy you were prepared to submit to the laws of men, and to the idea that men have of female virtue. The greater power is yours. You hold the two ends of life.

"Lan-ying, perhaps you feel that we have already known a physical happiness greater than we could have hoped, that when I brought you back to life we had achieved the highest communion. It is not possible to fall back into the ordinary.

"Perhaps if you agreed to return to the world, it could be with the goal of teaching me to communicate with you. Not only with the body but with the soul. Like the holy stranger, you believe in the soul, which doesn't deteriorate or age, which is the only thing to defy time. There are so many things between man and woman that are not spoken and that cry out to be spoken. What needs saying is infinite even if eternity goes on forever. Are you waiting for me to be ready for this dialogue before giving me a sign?

"Lan-ying, perhaps because of your belief in reincarnation, you don't want to spoil the chance of another life. You're waiting for this other life before starting over. No, not starting over—that's not right—starting afresh. In this other life, we won't have to wait until so close to the end to be together. We will be together from the first look and the first smile, and never part. An entire life to love in full recognition of what it means to love.

"Forgive me for all these thoughts. I don't know whether I'm right or wrong. I have given up soothsaying. Now I listen only to the voice of the heart. I am lost in ignorance. Tell me, if you know the answer: What does Heaven hold in store for us?"

Twenty-four

FOLLOWING THE FESTIVAL OF THE MOON CAME THAT OF THE
Double Nine (ninth day of the ninth month), marking the height
of autumn. Visitors stayed on the mountain to breathe the fresh
air and to cut *zhu-yu* branches as a sign of confidence in the
progress of the seasons. The year began its descent into hiber-
nation. The cold advanced gradually. The trees shed their
leaves, their branches tracing crude calligraphy in the uni-
formly gray sky. Each day life became more of a trial. When
winter finally arrived, someone needed to clear away the snow
from the paths leading to the well, whose iced surface had to
be broken before the buckets could draw water.

Winter had its charms. Nearby the monastery was the Cave of
the Immortals, where in summer pilgrims came in large numbers to burn incense and to drink water from the source. In the
dead of winter, as if to console mankind for its deprivations,
the cave became magical, for a curtain of crystal was formed
by the stalactites. From inside, one could look through this
curtain at the whiteness stretching beyond sight, whiteness

within which darted flames of blue and pink, as alive as the fires of summer. Here, a soul in pain might hear a voice whispering in his ear: "Everything transforms. There is beauty even in the heart of desolation."

Inside the monastery, fires were kept going in the prayer room and in the communal room. The bedrooms, however, were unheated. Propped against the pillow, fully dressed, beneath a thick cotton blanket, Dao-sheng struggled with the long winter nights. He had lost the vigor of youth and now was sensitive to even the smallest change in temperature. The hardest moment came between the fourth watch and dawn, when sleep left him and the cold grew most intense. That's when he took out the embroidered cloth and squeezed it to release its scent. He thought of the fish, of its life among the aquatic plants, its nearing the flower, orchid or lotus. A sensuous flow enveloped his body, bringing warmth and peace. He believed that the soul of Lan-ying had come to join with his.

The perfumed handkerchief that he had possessed long ago had been the object of feverish caresses. The hand that caressed this cloth was touching heart, not skin. Feeling not desire but consolation, he waited for dawn. He feared those dreams that had become more real and left him gasping when he awoke. There was that time when Xiao-fang told him that Lady Ying was waiting for him in the courtyard. The plum trees had blossomed during the night, and she had proposed that together they go to admire them in the snow. He had breathlessly agreed and gotten out of bed, straightened his clothes, and walked toward the door. Then realized it had been a dream.

Yet the plum trees really were in bloom. Their trembling petals announced the arrival of spring, the season that deepened the old wound, the hole in his heart that opened and closed, wept or bled. He forced himself to remember that there was work to be done on the monastery's walls and roof. The garden needed planting.

Little by little, the hole filled with something, though Dao-sheng couldn't describe what it was, and didn't try. Perhaps a combination of self-pity, disappointment, acceptance, and, strange though it might seem, happiness. Yes, happiness. Not fulfilling joy—affirmation of a pain felt many times before.

It was recognition of what had happened to him, to Lan-ying, to them both—of which this mountain and that valley and everything in this vast land were witnesses. What Dao-sheng had lived was undeniably exceptional. He was still waiting, but for now he could tell himself that he was waiting . . . for nothing. Everything was within. To find it all, he had only to look inward. Lan-ying was more alive to him than ever.

He stopped talking to himself. His words became part of an ongoing conversation with her—unhurried, uninhibited, conspiratorial. While washing the vegetables he might say, "Lan-ying, look how fresh these *wo-ju* are. And so early in the season!"

And she would reply, "All you have to do is add a few bamboo shoots and some chives. Everyone loves that."

At lunch, he would lift his rice-filled bowl and murmur his ritual thanks. He always heard a reply no one else did. "It is thanks to Buddha."

There was no doubting now that the woman had become the most intimate and most alive part of him. He was absorbed in the certitude that he was born in her, that he had grown up in her, and that he lived and would live forever in her—her look, her voice, her flesh, and her indefinable perfume, more secret than that of the lotus. She had become mother, sister, lover—it didn't matter, for she was the embodiment of the feminine, which the Taoists know as the Original Valley: Fecundity without end, opening to the infinite. There one can endure cold and ice, thirst and hunger, distance and delay, because there is the certitude that the promised happiness has always ever been there. Yes, that was it. Already there. Without that feeling, would Lan-ying have practiced charity? Would the stranger have risked his life? To others this might seem an illusion. There, to those who live it, life gets its true meaning. The fulfillment of desire resides within the desire itself. Dao-sheng made this idea his. Everything else was meaningless.

By degrees, he turned into the contemplator of a mystical passion that ended in him and at the same time lay ahead of him. Sitting alone on the wall bordering the kitchen garden, he no longer saw his shadow in an enclosed space. He was instead witness to this couple that was Lan-ying and Dao-sheng, who perhaps incarnated the law that drew those stars together every year. In more earthly terms, perhaps they were like two mulberry trees, their interlocking roots drawing nourishment from the same underground spring, perpetuating the earth's immemorial hope, which is never to be unbound. Or perhaps, even more incredibly, they were like those ethereal beings that are no longer divisible, for they are as flawless as the Primordial Breath—the mist that climbs the valley, crosses the layers of grain, and rejoins the clouds floating high above. These clouds will eventually turn into rain and replenish the land. The setting sun does not evaporate them; it reveals that they inhabit two realms, the visible and invisible, finite and infinite, connected by that which ceaselessly rushes between them.

On the fifteenth day of the eighth month, the Festival of the Moon came again. Gan-er asked again when they would see Lady Ying.

"Soon," replied Dao-sheng. "Or in a long time. It is a question I no longer ask. We already are together, as together as we would be if we saw one another. In this life and in another life, souls are joined, never to separate. Of that Lady Ying is sure. As for me, I am certain enough of it to live day by day. They say that your mother is no longer in this world. In appearance she is not there. In reality she has never left you. Where you go, she is there, more than ever."

Intended to help Gan-er, Dao-sheng's words indicated that he had entered a level in which resurgent hope and the end of waiting were reconciled. There was no more fear or anxiety. He was therefore able to devote himself fully to monastic tasks and feel detached. His strength continued to diminish; his face grew thinner; the strange light generated by an extenuated heart deepened the eyes and turned his skin darker. The others noticed these changes. He cared little. After all the quests and troubles of his life the passionate creature within his soul had become a pebble—beaten, polished, indestructible.

With the approach of another winter came premature cold weather—the chill wind and endless rain affected the health of several of the older monks. Then it was Dao-sheng's turn to become ill. He developed a cough.

One morning at the beginning of the second month, on his

way back from the well, Gan-er saw the first plum blossoms appearing along the steepest part of the path.

"Hah! About time spring came!" His whoops of joy preceded his arrival in his master's room. Seeing that Dao-sheng's eyes were half-closed and that he appeared lost in meditation, Gan-er started to back out. Dao-sheng reassured him, saying that it was time he got up. People would soon be coming to the monastery seeking consultation.

Dao-sheng began the habit of lying down in the afternoon, then rising toward twilight to join in the collective prayer. After this, he remained alone in his room. He took pleasure at the sight of the distant valley, which the setting sun bathed in soothing light. A path meandered through it. At the end of it, Dao-sheng was sitting behind a screen. Lan-ying approached him with light steps, her natural grace banishing sadness. She stopped and stood before his table. "I have made you wait a long time," she said. "Now at last we can see each other again."

That same night, a candle in his hand, Dao-sheng returned to his room after the evening meal. Dazzled by the brightness of the moonlight streaming through the shutters, he blew out the candle and set it on the table. He turned toward the bed and found it surrounded by female figures. They turned to face him. He recognized Xiao-fang, who with tears in her eyes motioned to him. He stepped closer and on the bed saw Lan-ying, sleeping, her face lit by that luminous goodness upon which recipients of her charity used to remark.

Dao-sheng couldn't tell whether this vision lasted for an instant or an eternity. He fell to his knees by the side of the bed.

The next day, he spoke to Gan-er.

"Gather together your things. We are going to see Lady Ying."

"That's wonderful news! We're going to see Lady Ying!"

"Yes, that's right. While her body is still in this world."

"Master, what do you mean?"

"Gan-er, listen to me well. Lady Ying's soul visited me last night to tell me of her departure. That's what I understood. We have to go down the mountain."

After taking leave of the other monks, who were astounded by the suddenness of this decision, Dao-sheng, followed by Gan-er, started down the mountain path, using a long stick as a cane. Winter had just ended, and the pilgrims had only barely cleared the path; progress was painfully slow.

From the very start he had felt a weakness overtake him, a weakness that came from a body worked too long from within, and from a heart that had given everything it had. They didn't make it halfway down until noon. Feeling dizzy, Dao-sheng looked for a place to rest and saw that great flat rock on the side of the path, the one from which one could observe the whole valley. It was covered with needles from the ancient pine towering above. Here was an old friend. He remembered sitting there once—but when? Ah yes! So long ago that it felt like another lifetime. But it was when he had started down the mountain and gone to the town. That was when it had all begun.

He threw aside his stick and hunched over to sit down, using his hands to guide him. Catching his breath, he turned to his disciple. "As you can see, Gan-er, I can't go any further. Go below and find a chair to carry me."

Alone after Gan-er left, Dao-sheng leaned back against the

trunk of the pine tree. Though breathing was difficult, he felt better. Once more he looked down at the valley. On the horizon there seemed to rise a plume of blue smoke. Afternoon had come. With the smell of pine and the hum of bees, the season was beginning its cycle of new promises. Between sky and earth, between the clouds moving past and the gathering hills endlessly revolved the rhythmic breathing, which the eagles soaring high above translated into wonderful arabesques. A final and supreme lucidity came to him.

Ah, this abounding and brightly colored world, with all its magnificent expanse! Still we come into it seeking one face. Once we have seen this face, it cannot be forgotten. Without it, the world offers neither flavor nor sense. Yet with this face everything assumes that flavor and that sense. Without our beloved, everything is dispersed. With our beloved, everything joins. In this life and the other life, as long as life is life . . .

Dizziness overpowered Dao-sheng, and this time it would not relent. He closed his eyes, perhaps never to open them again. At that very moment the third eye opened, the eye of Wisdom, which can stare down the infinite and proclaim in a firm voice, "Now we are together, Lan-ying. Of course we already have been for a long time, but that time has been fraught with troubles and fears and wounds and roughness and false joys and remorse. Let's enter the mystery of pure outpouring, pure exchange. For that, all of life has to be crossed over. We have learned to be together. Now we have to live what has been learned, indefinitely, regrets washed away, absence filled. Eternity is not too much. I am coming!"

Of this great and vast world, Dao-sheng heard nothing more

and had no further need to hear. Yet a voice still rose from the valley. It was that of the faithful Gan-er.

"Master," he cried, "the messenger from the convent has come! We're going up!"

Author's Note

I BEGAN WRITING THIS WORK IN NOVEMBER 2000 AT THE VILLA Mont-Noir, the regional residential center for European writers. I benefited from the particularly favorable working conditions there, and would like here to express my gratitude.